Billionaire Twin Surgeons

*Worlds collide at the exclusive
Thorncroft Royal Infirmary!*

When a specialist case for a VIP client sees
estranged twins Basilius and Henrik Jansen forced
to work together at the ultraluxurious Thorncroft
Royal Infirmary, tensions reach fever pitch.

But as Bas discovers his one night with stranger
Naomi had consequences, and Rik goes toe-to-toe
with the distractingly beautiful Grace, it's not just
saving lives that has their hearts racing…

Read Bas and Naomi's story,
Shock Baby for the Doctor

And Rik and Grace's story,
Forbidden Nights with the Surgeon

Both available now!

Dear Reader,

I can never predict how a story may slide into my brain. Sometimes it's the spark of a scene, perhaps the meet-cute, perhaps the big black moment. Other times it can be the heroine or the hero themselves. In this Billionaire Twin Surgeons duet—my nineteenth and twentieth books!—it was the idea of the twin heroes themselves.

Henrik "Rik" Magnusson/Jansen has spent decades searching for the brother who was torn away from him when they were just kids. It never occurred to him that his brother wouldn't be interested in any kind of reunion.

Enter strong, principled Grace. It was bittersweet to watch her wrangle with her ever-growing attraction for Rik versus her sense of loyalty to her best friend—who also happens to be Rik's brother.

This story was a blast to write, and I only hope you love both these billionaire twins—and their sassy, fearless heroines—as much as I do.

I love hearing from my readers, so feel free to drop by my site at www.charlotte-hawkes.com or pop over to Facebook or Twitter @chawkesuk.

I can't wait to meet you.

Charlotte x

FORBIDDEN NIGHTS WITH THE SURGEON

CHARLOTTE HAWKES

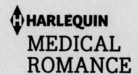

HARLEQUIN

MEDICAL
ROMANCE

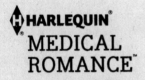

HARLEQUIN®
MEDICAL
ROMANCE™

Recycling programs
for this product may
not exist in your area.

ISBN-13: 978-1-335-40926-3

Forbidden Nights with the Surgeon

Copyright © 2022 by Charlotte Hawkes

Harlequin Enterprises ULC
22 Adelaide St. West, 41st Floor
Toronto, Ontario M5H 4E3, Canada
www.Harlequin.com

Printed in U.S.A.

Born and raised on the Wirral Peninsula in England, **Charlotte Hawkes** is mom to two intrepid boys who love her to play building block games with them and who object loudly to the amount of time she spends on the computer. When she isn't writing—or building with blocks—she is company director for a small Anglo/French construction firm. Charlotte loves to hear from readers, and you can contact her at her website: charlotte-hawkes.com.

Books by Charlotte Hawkes

Harlequin Medical Romance

Royal Christmas at Seattle General
The Bodyguard's Christmas Proposal

Reunited on the Front Line
Second Chance with His Army Doc
Reawakened by Her Army Major

A Summer in São Paolo
Falling for the Single Dad Surgeon

The Army Doc's Baby Secret
Unwrapping the Neurosurgeon's Heart
Surprise Baby for the Billionaire
The Doctor's One Night to Remember
Reunited with His Long-Lost Nurse
Tempted by Her Convenient Husband

Visit the Author Profile page
at Harlequin.com for more titles.

Derek

I love you enough to let you talk over songs
on my playlist…

(but not every time—let's not push it).

xxx

CHAPTER ONE

HENRIK 'RIK' MAGNUSSON—or Henrik Jansen, as he supposed he should call himself, now that he knew that to be his real name—cast his eye around the ballroom of the opulent venue that was hosting tonight's exclusive medical gala, and his eye caught her straight away.

The arresting stranger was standing within a small group, smiling politely, a part of it and yet somehow not. She wore a long blue-grey ball gown with a plunging neckline that nonetheless only offered brief, tantalising glimpses of what lay beyond. No more than any other woman in the room—decidedly less, in fact—and yet he couldn't seem to stop staring.

And when she lifted her eyes and looked right at him—as though some sixth sense had compelled her to do—Rik couldn't find a way to drag his gaze away.

But he had to.

Because he wasn't here to be distracted. And because he hadn't earned his hated reputation as *den iskalla Munk*—the stone-cold monk—for nothing.

A split second later, though he couldn't have said how, his focus was back where it belonged—namely, in the architecturally stunning room.

The place was unequivocally magnificent, from its stone columns to the vaulted, ornately crafted stone ceiling, some twenty-five feet above their heads. Clearly no expense had been spared with the opulent décor, with flower garlands wound lovingly around the pillars, the ornate iron fretwork and over the expansive arched doorways.

Even the big band playing flawlessly on the dais couldn't have been more perfectly selected for the occasion. The architecture of the room enhanced the acoustics spectacularly.

But it was the guest list that was even more striking.

The ballroom heaved and swelled with the monied and influential, all of whom were here because it was the place to be seen, rather than because of any deeply held charitable values. These people were only eager to part with their money if it meant they were the subject of a sharp, media-bound photograph with the gala's keynote speaker—the eminent plastic surgeon to the stars, Magnus Jansen. Or perhaps with his rising star surgeon son, Basilius Jansen.

Whilst Rik himself remained, well…if not invisible—it was impossible to stay unnoticed given his six-foot-three, blond-haired Viking appearance attracting admiring glances wherever he went—then at least *anonymous*. Certainly no one here had any idea that he, too, was a Jansen.

And how would they? Indeed, for thirty-six

years—up until six months ago, in fact—neither had he.

As far as the world was concerned, there were only two Jansen miracle men. The renowned Magnus Jansen, who headlined for his skill both as a surgeon and as a playboy, and his son Bas, who the media feverishly declared had come for his father's crown on both counts.

Either way, there was no second son. No third Jansen. Bas—it was universally agreed—had broken the mould.

Rik knew that even if he got up on that stage and declared who he was to the entire ballroom, no one would believe that he was the young Lothario surgeon's brother.

People certainly wouldn't believe that he was Bas's long-lost twin—and not just because they weren't identical.

Besides, he would never do something as wild as declaring it to everyone. That kind of impulsive, spirited daring had never been him. There had only ever been room for one wild, crazy Magnusson brother—as they'd both once believed they were—with a flair for the dramatic, Rik thought with a pang of nostalgia. And that person had always been Bas.

A low punch walloped into Rik's gut, as he weaved an efficient path around the room. It seemed that even the mere name of his beloved, long-lost brother echoed through the neural pathways of his mind much as an ethereal spirit might haunt the corridors of some medieval castle. It conjured up dusty memories of a childhood that Rik could never really have described as 'happy', but which—thanks to Mrs P, and Bertie, and the irrepressible Bas himself—had nonetheless offered some happier moments. Some love.

The past almost thirty years had been notably lacking in either. He'd had friends, of course, and girlfriends at uni, but that visceral loss he'd felt as a seven-year-old meant that he'd never felt truly able to let anyone in completely. He'd been trapped in some dark dungeon of his mother's creation. Because, as far as Erin Sundberg was concerned, why should she be the only one to suffer if she could cause pain to those around her, too?

Had it not been for Bas, Rik knew he would have cut Erin out of his life. The same day that his fifteen-year-old self had finally had enough of being his stepfather's punchbag, and had walked out of the so-called family home once and for all. The only reason he hadn't turned his back on Erin completely had been because he'd been desperately hoping for just one scrap of information from her that might help him to finally track down the brother he'd always idolised as a kid.

And still, she had deliberately said nothing. Raising him as a *Magnusson*—wilfully letting him search for Bas *Magnusson* for the better part of three decades—had just been the tip of her deception, not that he'd realised it at the time. And then a year ago, she'd finally died, taking her secrets to her grave—snuffing out his hopes in the cruellest act of all.

Another circuit of the ballroom completed, Rik moved up the luxuriously carpeted stairs to survey the floor beyond, shocked when his eyes instinctively sought out that tall vision in blue-grey from before.

Since when had he believed in self-sabotage? That wasn't his style. He was more renowned for his dogged determination. Even if Bas wasn't here—and Rik was beginning to suspect that he wasn't—was that any reason to let himself be distracted?

This time, however, instead of snatching his focus back to the room, Rik found his eyes lingering on the figure. Allowing his gaze to track down as he took in the narrow blue velvet ribbon belt that circled a waist that his hands suddenly itched to span, before falling away to a full flowing skirt that skimmed the polished wooden floor as she moved.

More than that, those movements made her sparkle captivatingly—and Rik feared it had nothing to do with the subtle, glittery patterns, almost like fireworks, that shimmered as she moved.

Den iskalla Munk, he reproved himself tacitly—coldly—dragging his eyes away once more, ignoring the fact that this time it was even harder to do so than last time.

How could he be distracted tonight, of all nights? Being here was supposed to be about finally reconnecting with the brother he'd thought he'd never see again.

As if that could somehow kick-start the life Rik felt had been on hold, all these years.

With Bas gone, it was as if the light had been snuffed out in his little seven-year-old's world. He had frozen over. And that thing in his chest that most people called a heart had initially petrified. Then, as the decades had marched inexorably by, it had ultimately crumbled, leaving a nothingness in its wake.

Stone-cold, indeed. Rik knew it, and in a twisted way he welcomed it.

Far better to have shut himself off, than to have the people he loved snatched from him, one by one. Mrs P. Bertie. Bas.

He had never dreamed that there could be a chance to resurrect anything from that petrified dust.

Shaking off the odd, unfamiliar feelings, Rik tried to keep his focus on the ball.

Indeed, if it hadn't been for a chance encounter six months back, he would still have no idea of the Jansen connection, even now. No idea that Magnus Jansen was his father—not *somebody*

Magnusson—and no idea that he should be looking for Bas *Jansen*.

That one nugget of information had been enough to allow Rik to finally track them down. And even though his letters to Bas hadn't been returned, it hadn't stopped Rik from making his way here—both to the UK, and to this monied medical ball—where the hospital grapevine had led him to believe that his now playboy brother would be guaranteed to attend.

Yet there was no sign of Bas anywhere. It seemed another circuit of the room was in order.

Dropping back down the steps, Rik moved skilfully through the crowd as it swelled and heaved, deftly avoiding the flirtatious women stepping into his path. He didn't need the distraction, and one-night stands had never been his style.

He'd seen from the cradle just what they could do. His mother flaunting her indiscretions to get a rise out of his stepfather, which had invariably resulted in the angry drunk taking it out on him and Bas and then, once Bas had gone—just him.

It was why he'd decided long ago that he would never, *never* permit anyone, or anything, to get under his skin. Even as a kid, Rik had known he'd begun to turn into himself, just as Bas had begun to act out.

Now, thirty years on, Rik was beginning to learn that not a lot seemed to have changed. His brother was apparently still daring—a fun, coveted playboy—whilst he himself had his own decidedly less scandalous reputations.

Aside from the Stone Monk, he was known as *den ishand kirurg*—the ice-hand surgeon. Because his hand never shook, and he never made a mistake.

So why did tonight feel like a bomb inside him, waiting to explode?

Dragging himself back to the moment, Rik decided to make one more sweep of the ballroom, and if there was still no sign of Bas, then he would return to his hotel suite upstairs, and he would try to find his brother again, in the morning.

However much the idea frustrated him.

Executing a sharp about-turn, Rik ploughed a fresh path through the parting throng. From the snippets of conversation he was catching, it appeared that he wasn't the only one to be speculating on the party-loving Bas Jansen's unexpected absence.

So much for tonight's reconciliation. It was time to cut his losses and leave.

'Excuse me,' he muttered automatically as someone stepped into his path.

Another woman wearing the familiar expression that inevitably meant she was keen to introduce herself to him. Rik smiled and returned the greeting, before expertly disengaging himself, but as he moved her aside and continued his striding to the exit, he might have known that flash of blue-grey would, once again, seize his attention.

Before he could stop himself, he had turned. Looked. And this time, there was no fighting the attraction that had been arcing between them from that first shared glance.

It shot through him like a thousand volts. Only somehow thrilling, rather than deadly.

A plethora of thoughts crowded his usually logical brain, but the one that pounded in his mind loudest of all was that he'd been right. That shimmering, dazzling, breathtaking light wasn't coming from her sparkling dress—it was a brilliance that was all hers. A lustre. *She* was the real draw. The reason he couldn't seem to drag his gaze away. The reason he didn't want to.

Without even knowing what he was doing, Rik plunged back into the crowd, and it didn't matter that he lost sight of her for a moment because his body suddenly seemed to have an inbuilt compass, and it was heading directly to her.

It was almost a relief when the stranger disappeared into the swell of guests, Grace Henley told herself, as she fought to remember how to breathe again.

It was an unsettling experience. Hadn't she made herself immune to any man years ago? Near enough a decade and a half ago, to be a little more precise.

And yet the impact of this particular man's gaze had landed on her like a net around a butterfly, trapping her without even having to touch her. Just as it had that first time. And the second. Not that she was much of a butterfly, more like a wallflower.

Even so, each time he'd emerged from the crowd—each time his eyes had seemed to find hers—she hadn't been able to move, or breathe, or even blink.

And then he'd disappeared, and the net cage around her had simply…evaporated.

Grace glanced surreptitiously at her watch for the hundredth time already that night and gave herself a half-grin, half-grimace.

It was finally time that she could make her excuses and leave—not that anyone was likely to be bothered. She wouldn't have even been at the ball had Bas—the closest thing she'd ever had to a best friend—not demanded it of her. Some cryptic request to look out for 'anything unusual'.

But there was nothing unusual about this gala. It was as predictably magnificent and depressing as ever. She would far rather be in the operating room saving mums and babies than networking with a bunch of people who thought money and the latest designer accessories were matters of life and death.

It was only Bas who had made these things fun for her. Even if it was just her amusement at watching him fend off the advances of a multitude of women throwing themselves—sometimes quite literally—at one half of the eminent Jansen duo.

Look up playboy surgeon on any Internet search, and a picture of Bas or Magnus, or even both of them, would surely appear.

But there was another side to Bas, her friend. A side that was raw, and sad, but fiercely loyal. And she'd thought it was perhaps that friendship that she'd miss the most when she finally left Thorncroft Royal Infirmary.

She'd planned to share her plan tonight. To explain that she'd recently begun to feel restless. Unsettled. That her reason for coming here—coming *back* here, if she was going to be strictly accurate—had begun to fade, and that there was a part of her—a guilty, secretive slither inside her—that had begun to think it was time to move somewhere other than Thorncroft.

Though she couldn't tell Bas why. She'd never been able to share that long-buried secret with anyone. Perhaps it was the sheer, crushing pressure of it that had finally convinced her that it was time to go.

So, tonight was supposed to have been the night she'd been going to broach it with him. She'd rehearsed her speech so many times. And then he'd called with the most startling news she thought she'd ever heard. That he was about to become a father.

The irony of it hadn't been lost on Grace.

But there'd been no time to dwell. Worse than that—far worse—had been the fact that she'd been the one to have to tell the accidental couple that there was something wrong with their baby. No parent wanted to hear that their baby was going to need complex surgery within days of its birth.

God, it had just been a horrific night, all around. The sooner she got home, to a hot shower, a light movie, and her cat, the better. And she didn't care what that made her sound like.

Taking her leave from the cluster of guests around her—who had only really stopped to talk to her because they'd wanted to know where the 'incredible Bas' was—Grace turned with relief, ducked her head and hurried away.

Straight into some unyielding, muscled wall of a man.

'Oof.' Her breath was knocked out of her, even as a pair of strong hands reached out to steady her.

'*Ursåkta mig.* Excuse me.'

By the way her blood pressure was affected, she didn't need to lift her head to guess who the man was.

'Sorry...that was... I wasn't looking where I was going,' she blurted out awkwardly.

'Don't be sorry.'

But his voice was muffled somehow. Distant. It took her a moment to process that it might have something to do with the fact that she was still held against a solid, hot, unmistakeably male chest.

Sinfully defined.

Grace felt her palms begin to actually itch with the effort of not reaching out to touch it. She lifted her head slowly, so slowly, and half wished she hadn't. And it was impossible to say what affected her most. The electricity that arced through her at his touch, the exquisitely low rumble of his sensual male voice, or the breath-stealing masculine beauty of what had to be one of the most stunning men she'd ever seen in her life.

Seeing him from a distance had been one thing, but up close was a whole different experience. And she didn't feel like a wallflower any longer— not with this stunning man staring down at her.

The man who had been causing a series of rumblings through much of the female contingency of tonight's illustrious guest list. No wonder a dozen or so pairs of baleful, heavily fake-lashed eyes were launching sharp, invisible daggers into her from all sides.

And still, Grace couldn't seem to move her body. To escape. So, instead, she allowed herself to indulge for a moment.

The man was six-foot-three, at a guess, and incredibly well-built, with broad shoulders and a strong neck, not too thick. He looked like some kind of model and, in a way, she hoped he was.

The last thing Thorncroft Royal Infirmary needed, she decided, with some inexplicable degree of maniacal amusement, was another wild Lothario like Bas. The man might be the closest thing she'd ever had to a best friend, but she wasn't oblivious to the trail of broken hearts in his wake.

Two heartbreakers would be more than the hospital—than the entire county—could possibly cope with.

And still, she couldn't seem to drag her eyes from his. She felt pinned to the spot, barely able to breathe let alone move—though the rest of the ballroom seemed to have faded into nothingness.

Her pulse hammered hectically in her neck, at her wrists, and somewhere else—somewhere lower, however much she tried to deny it—and whatever she might try, Grace knew there was no calming it. As long as this man's gaze was on her, its chaotic pace was beyond her control.

Like something she might have read about in one of those thrilling magazine stories she'd sneakily read as a kid—before her academic of a mother had thrown them out, loftily reminding her that she had a whole library of far more intellectually stimulating journals and classical masterpieces to choose from. As if it had been the Great Library of Alexandria, rather than the book collection right there in the front room of their bland, suburban, three-bedroom family house.

But, right in this instant, Grace couldn't think of a single one of those dusty tomes that could possibly have been more stimulating than whatever it was that she was pretending she wasn't feeling just now.

This scraping, shimmering thrill that made her body feel as though it was more awake than it had ever been in her life before. And then, he spoke.

'Can I buy you a drink?'

Inexplicably, the corners of her mouth tugged upwards despite her suddenly jangling nerves.

'It's an open bar.'

Why had she said that?

Grace frowned—though whether at her own gaucheness or at her uncharacteristic reaction to the stranger, she couldn't quite be sure. She should have just accepted. Now she looked as though she wasn't interested.

Which, of course, she wasn't.

So why was she still standing in front of him? Waiting?

Everything about the man screamed wealth and power, which meant that he was most likely a wealthy guest. A man accustomed to getting exactly what he wanted, when he wanted it. The kind of man with whom she definitely didn't want to share her future.

Grace blinked abruptly.

Since when had she started to think of sharing her life with someone again?

That was a dream that she'd let go of when she was sixteen—in that one year that had changed everything. The year she never talked about. The year she was never allowed to talk about.

Was this all part of the way everything had been shifting inside her recently? Could it be that her decision to leave Thorncroft meant that she was finally ready to let go of the past, and move on with her life?

Obviously not with this stranger. But, after years of being the wallflower and watching other people have fun, maybe this was her place to start. A flirt and drink, at a party, with a handsome man, didn't seem a bad place to begin.

It certainly accounted for why she was still standing in the same spot, still staring at the beautiful stranger as she waited for the world to stop spinning and willing herself to say something. Anything. Though preferably something at least slightly witty.

'Do you work at Thorncroft Royal Infirmary?'
So, not witty at all, then. *Embarrassing.*

CHAPTER TWO

'I DO,' THE stranger answered seriously, as though her inquiry was perfectly acceptable.

It took Grace a moment to remember that she'd asked if he worked at the hospital with her. And try as she might, she couldn't stop herself from frowning again.

'I don't recognise you.'

His mouth curved up into a small smile of his own.

'Should I be flattered? Or do you know everyone who works at the hospital?'

'I wasn't trying to flatter you.'

'Yet there you go again.' He grinned.

And it was the strangest sensation, being teased by this man. Thrilling and terrifying all at once. But she hadn't fought her way to where she was now by being easily intimidated.

Lifting her head up, Grace met the full intensity of those mesmerising eyes—not quite green, but not entirely blue—head-on.

'What can I say?' She offered a delicate shrug. 'It seems I haven't been housebroken yet.'

It was the quirky, funny side of herself that few people ever saw. She usually repressed it around anyone except for her friend, Bas—certainly around strangers. It was impossible to say what it was about this man that made her feel so comfortable—and yet so damned *aware*—from this initial encounter.

For a split second, he simply looked at her, then the stranger threw back his head and let out a low, magnificent laugh.

And something warm and liquid-like slid smoothly through Grace.

'Clearly you haven't been working here long, though,' she noted evenly, trying not to feel so ridiculously victorious as his head cocked to one side when he studied her a little more carefully.

'What makes you say that?'

'Because the hospital grapevine at this place is alive and flourishing. If you'd been here for more than a minute, it would definitely have been buzzing with gossip about you.'

He grinned at her, and it burst inside her like fireworks. Sparkling around her and raining down excitement.

'Ah, but you don't even know that I'm a good enough surgeon to warrant discussion. Or a bad enough one, for that matter.'

She narrowed her gaze.

'I didn't even know that you were a surgeon,' she pointed out. 'I'm simply stating that new faces equal new discussion. But I think you already knew that.'

She certainly wasn't going to highlight the fact that having a new surgeon who could easily moonlight as a London billboard model would make the interest in him even more feverish.

'*Faktiskt?*' He arched his brow. 'Indeed? And am I to take *that* to be a compliment?'

She shrugged elegantly.

'Take it however you want,' she quipped. 'I'm Grace Henley, by the way.'

She thrust her hand out, as though hoping the banality of it could somehow stifle the heat that had been building higher and higher between them, even during the course of the conversation. Though deep down, she suspected it wouldn't muffle anything at all. Least of all her inexplicably excited libido.

It was all so unlike her. So strange. So thrilling.

She cranked her polite smile up another notch.

Still, her heart seemed to hang for a fraction of a second when he paused before ultimately reaching out his own hand. And then, as electricity arced between them once again, so fast and so shocking, Grace was almost surprised when the gargantuan, grandiose chandeliers in the ballroom didn't flicker, and hum, and then explode.

'Rik Magnusson,' he introduced himself, his voice little more than a low rumble like a lick against the softest part of her body. 'So, Grace Henley, if I can't buy you a drink then the least I can do is inject a little fun into your evening. Do you dance?'

'I…do,' she heard herself answer before her mind had time to engage.

Some atypical, spontaneous devil sneaking out of her without warning.

The only other person to ever make her see her fun, wild streak had been Bas. But this—Rik—was a whole different level of sinful. She could feel it in her bones.

Lower, actually. If she was going to be entirely truthful with herself.

'Good.' His voice rumbled through her as he spun her around and guided her to the dance floor simply by the lightest of touches from his hand at the small of her back. 'Then enough talking. Let's dance.'

And though she meant to say no, she found herself being guided across the ballroom, the palm of his head searing into the small of her back, and then swept into his arms as they danced into the beat of the big band.

It was like some kind of dream, or perhaps a fairy tale, Grace thought, rather breathlessly, a lifetime later. Or perhaps it had only been minutes, who could tell? Though if glowers were scalpels she would have had a hundred of them embedded between her shoulder blades right now.

But when he held her body against his, his heat seeming to seep right through every layer of dermis to permeate her very bones, she couldn't seem to care the way she knew she ought to. It was all still something of a blur and she thought perhaps she was still waiting for the whole world to tilt completely and go spinning off its axis.

There was something so inescapably beautiful, mesmerising even, about him.

A study in masculinity that even Rodin would have ached to capture in bronze. And it made her feel unsteady inside, as if she'd been scooped out and left hollow. Grace couldn't explain it, but the longer he spun her around the ballroom floor, the edgier, the more thrilling the sensation that wound through her.

Surely she ought to do something—anything— to mute it.

'So, how long have you been at Thorncroft?'

Amusement danced within those green-blue eyes and…something else. Something she couldn't quite identify. She might have thought… *wariness*? But that didn't seem to fit.

'Is this to be our discussion this evening?'

'We have to talk about something,' she retorted, though there was an uncharacteristic shake to her voice.

Fortunately, he didn't know her well enough to notice. Or perhaps it was that, whilst he spoke English fluently, the hint of an accent indicated that it wasn't his native language. It reminded her of the accent Bas put on when he knew it would make women puddle at his feet.

'Do you know Bas Jansen?'

'Pardon?'

Was it her imagination, or was his voice sharper than before?

'Or Magnus?' she guessed, instead.

'Magnus?'

Did his step falter for a split second as they danced?

'Magnus Jansen,' she clarified, watching him a little more carefully this time. More prepared.

'What makes you think that?'

But this time there was nothing. He seemed quite relaxed.

Too relaxed? a voice in her head asked, before she dismissed the foolish notion.

'I don't know.' She shook her head, a rueful smile creeping over her. 'I just thought…the faint accent, the name, the somewhat Viking appearance.'

'By Viking, do you mean slightly dishevelled, with battle scars, and kohl-framed eyes?'

And there it was again. He was teasing her, yet there was an almost imperceptible edge to his voice that she couldn't quite explain.

'I meant more your…what six-foot-three, six-foot-four height?' Dammit, she hadn't intended to sound so fan-girlish. 'Your blond hair, and your green-blue eyes.'

Not to mention the fact that he was so well-built that it was only too embarrassingly easy to imagine him hauling her over his shoulder and carrying her off into the night. He had such thrillingly broad shoulders, it could happily take a woman a lifetime to explore them properly.

'Know many Vikings, do you?'

What was it about him that made her wish she'd never started this line of conversation?

'Well, like I said, there's Magnus Jansen. And there's his son, Bas.'

'And they look like me, do they?' His voice whispered down her spine, but she still couldn't explain it.

'Not exactly,' she answered carefully. 'They're both tall, too, but they have almost white-blond hair. Yours is more a dirty blond.'

'Is that right? Dirty blond...' he echoed, some-how making it sound ridiculously sexy.

Grace plunged on desperately.

'Plus, they don't have any accent, of course. Unless Bas is seducing a woman who's making him work for it.'

'I've only been here a day and already I've heard a lot about Bas Jansen. He has quite the reputation for burning the candle at both ends.'

'Bas has a..."work hard, play hard" ethos,' she conceded with a smile. 'He's certainly a brilliant surgeon.'

'With a legion of female suitors, I believe.' Rik's expression darkened.

Was he jealous? One alpha male studying an-other alpha male? Grace fought back a wave of disappointment. He hadn't seemed the type, but there was no doubt that he was interested in learning about Bas.

'I'm sure you'll agree that what a person does in their own time is their business, just as long as they are professional in their working life. Whatever rumours you've heard about Bas Jansen are just that, rumours.'

Which she thought was a fairly decent speech, given that her head was still scrambled from the feel of Rik's arms around her, still swirling her around the dance floor,

'You're very defensive of Bas,' he noted. 'Are you one of his admirers?'

'I'm his friend,' Grace retorted, telling herself to stop there. Reminding herself that anything more was none of this man's business. '*Just* his friend.'

And she wondered why she felt the need to put quite so much emphasis into it.

'Is that so?'

There was a lift to his tone that thrilled her even as she tried to pretend it didn't. Even as she forced herself to concentrate on her dancing, and her footwork, rather than the solid feel of the man—the heat from his thighs—as their bodies moved so slickly together.

This was…ridiculous.

'It is so,' she muttered firmly. 'There has never been anything more between us.'

Namely because she'd been nineteen when she'd met him at her first year of her medical degree at university—and still numbed from what had happened only a few years earlier.

The fact that it had been Bas who had made her laugh for the first time in almost four years—a sound that had shocked her the first time she'd heard it after so long—was surely how he had become important to her, so quickly.

And the fact that she was possibly the first woman who hadn't toppled into lust with him was no doubt what had appealed to Bas, too. It didn't mean she hadn't noticed quite how beautiful a man he was, of course. It just meant that she'd been too shell-shocked to feel anything. Certainly to act on it.

And Grace was eternally glad that she hadn't, because if she had, then they would never have become the close friends they were today.

Nevertheless, it didn't stop people gossiping, or speculating that there was more to her relationship with Bas the playboy. And, as much as she might tell herself otherwise, she didn't want this particular man thinking the same.

'And there never will be anything more than friendship between Bas and me,' she added, before she could check herself.

Which had been the case before she'd decided it was time to leave Thorncroft for pastures new, and before Bas had found out that he was set to become a father.

Not that this man—*Rik*—needed to know any of that.

The music was coming to an end now, the band seamlessly moving from a waltz to a foxtrot, and Grace prepared for Rik to let her go. And of course it meant nothing that she couldn't decide whether she was relieved at that, or frustrated.

'Then it seems you're in the minority,' Rik commented, which she couldn't help thinking was neither accepting her word, nor refuting it.

She also noted that he wasn't letting her go, instead transitioning them both into a smooth foxtrot. And it didn't matter that she told herself the fluttering of her stomach was just nerves that she'd get the steps wrong, deep down she knew that wasn't the real reason.

It likely explained why her voice suddenly sounded so prim.

'That's as maybe. But it doesn't make it any less true. What's more interesting is your apparent interest in him.'

'You're right,' Rik noted abruptly, his expression rueful and his tone light again. 'It's my fault, not yours. It's simply that I'm here at Thorncroft Royal Infirmary because I've secured a place on the Jansen Surgical Exchange programme.'

'Ah, I see.' She nodded, understanding suddenly. 'You're trying to get to know the surgeons you think will be your bosses.'

'Mmm, something like that.'

It wasn't exactly a full-hearted agreement, but Grace was too preoccupied with her own thoughts. She couldn't help wondering what kind of surgeon Rik might be. Typically, anyone who won a place on the Jansen Surgical Exchange programme had to be good. More than good. They had to have the potential to alter the course of surgery in whatever their specialist field happened to be. Just as Magnus, and now Bas, were pioneers in the field of plastic surgery.

And with a face and body like Rik's, it wouldn't surprise her if he was one, too. It was certainly majestic enough to be a walking advert for flawless looks.

'What is your specialist field?' she asked abruptly.

He offered another rueful smile, as if he could read her thoughts.

'Plastic surgery.'

She laughed out loud.

'Of course it is.'

But at least that meant that he hadn't been acting like some weird, jealous alpha male before, checking out the competition for dating. He'd simply been acting as a competitive alpha surgeon—and that was something she could easily cope with. A man who was clearly dedicated to his career.

Looks aside, a healthy competitive streak when it came to work was something she found particularly attractive. The question was whether Rik had what it took to keep up with the Jansen pair.

Many didn't, yet there was something about Rik that made her think that he might even be able to give Magnus and Bas a run for their money. Or perhaps it was just that she wanted that to be the case. For his sake, of course. Nothing to do with her.

'Can I offer you a little advice?' She hesitated. Had Rik been anybody else, she was fairly sure that she wouldn't have said anything.

'I would welcome it,' he replied easily, allowing her to feel a little less tense.

'Don't listen to everything you hear from the hospital rumour mill. Yes, Bas has a reputation as a playboy, but that doesn't stop him from being a brilliant surgeon. There's a reason the Jansen name is so esteemed.'

'Because Magnus Jansen has been pioneering new surgical techniques, pushing the boundaries of what plastic surgeons can do, for the past three decades.'

No, she certainly wouldn't be telling anyone else what she was about to tell Rik.

'Magnus Jansen is a good surgeon. A *great* surgeon,' she corrected. 'There is no doubt that he pushed the boundaries of his field. But the advances attributed to the Jansen name from the last ten years have been Bas's. Any patient would be lucky to have Magnus as a surgeon, but Bas is the one you want to watch. He is the one you should spend the next few months learning from. If it hadn't been for him, I wouldn't be a doctor.'

For a long moment Rik was silent. But then, Grace didn't need his words in order to read every taut line in his body.

'You seem very defensive of him, for just a friend.'

Grace opened her mouth to explain herself, then changed her mind. The foxtrot was coming to an end and Rik was deliberately moving her out of his arms. Clearly, their dancing was over.

'Thank you for the dances, anyway.' She dredged up a bright smile.

It shouldn't feel like such a wrench. Especially since it somehow managed to irk her new acquaintance. She shouldn't want him to wrap his arms around her or pull her back in for another dance.

Yet, it was almost terrifying how badly she wanted precisely that.

'Enjoy the rest of your evening.' Rik dipped his head politely, but his smile—like hers, she feared—didn't quite match his eyes.

Whatever that tiny, exquisite seed had been between them—it was gone now.

'I'll be leaving anyway.'

'No need to leave on my account.'

His gaze trapped her in place, making her blurt out an explanation.

'I'm not. Of course I'm not. I was leaving anyway. I mean, I was just on my way to the exit when I bumped into you.'

Grace fought off another deep, giveaway blush. He didn't think she'd engineered their encounter deliberately, did he? She'd watched plenty of women crash into Bas accidentally on purpose in the past.

'Don't tell me you're Cinderella, and you have to leave the ball before midnight?' He was teasing her, but there was still an edge to it.

Still, she tried to smile again.

'I'm not Cinderella. But yes, I have to leave the ball. Or this gala fundraiser, anyway.'

He seemed to hesitate for a moment.

'Then I'll walk you out.'

She wanted, so badly, to accept. Instead, she offered a light shake of her head. Truth be told, she wanted far more than for him to just walk her out. Which was crazy, since she never did anything like that usually. It was one of the reasons she had such a reputation for being a little bit too much of a nerd.

Sometimes, it seemed that her reputation as a nerd grew in equal proportion to Bas's reputation as a playboy. As though it was her role, as his best friend, to balance him out.

But then if that were the case, given his current serious situation with Naomi, this was the time for her to cut loose and have a little fun, for once.

It was harder than it should have been to dismiss the notion as preposterous.

'Don't be silly, you should stay and enjoy yourself. The gala will go on for a few hours yet.'

'Not for me,' Rik told her, his hand pressed too distractingly against the small of her back as he guided her away from the dance floor. 'Believe it or not, I was leaving, too.'

She eyed him sceptically.

'You didn't look like you were leaving. You look like you are searching for someone.'

To her surprise, Rik's eyes darkened. Only a fraction, but it was there nonetheless. She certainly didn't expect him to answer.

'I was just looking out for Magnus. I thought I might introduce myself before formally meeting him on Monday. Only now, after what you've told me, perhaps I should also look out for Bas.'

It sounded perfectly logical, so why did she feel as though she was missing something? Grace dismissed the niggling thought. Surely it wasn't any of her business, anyway.

'Bas isn't here tonight.' She thought about her friend, and Naomi—the woman he'd just discovered was the mother of his child—and hoped they were doing okay. 'As for Magnus, he wouldn't thank you for introducing yourself. Especially not at a gala like this.'

She clamped her mouth shut, shocked at herself. No need to tell Rik that his new boss would be far more interested in any of the beautiful, eager women here tonight than in his newest surgeon.

She didn't customarily go around criticising colleagues, especially senior surgeons. Unless it was to Bas, of course. He had always been her sounding board for when hospital life frustrated her. Just as she'd been his sounding board for his all too exacting father.

Magnus might be a great surgeon, but he'd been sorely lacking as a parent.

What was it about Rik that had her almost sharing such personal information? Something she had never, *never* done before.

'I spoke out of turn.' She shut down the conversation. 'Forget about it. Anyway, goodnight, Rik. Thank you again for the dances.'

But as she turned to leave, she was acutely aware of Rik moving alongside her. His long, casual stride easily keeping pace with her. Apparently, she was going to have to wait a little longer to shake him.

If only her unexpectedly traitorous body weren't trying to tell her that shaking this man off was the last thing it wanted to do.

CHAPTER THREE

'ARE YOU A DOCTOR?' They were barely out of the ballroom before they were accosted by a concierge who was bustling their way. 'There's a woman giving birth in the lift.'

Grace knew the ideal response. It was drilled into them from almost the start of their medical careers—outside the hospital it was never advised to admit you were a doctor unless there was absolutely no choice. Too many well-intentioned doctors had been sued after attempting to help in an emergency.

But it went against everything she believed in.

She gritted her teeth.

'Where's the patient?'

This was about doing the right thing. And it absolutely wasn't influenced by wanting to put some space between herself and the too tempting man who had walked out of that ballroom beside her.

In an instant, her mind switched from the awkwardness of the evening, into clear, professional mode.

'This way.' The concierge looked past her, straight to Rik. 'We've phoned for an ambulance, but it isn't here yet. Follow me.'

'I'm not an obstetrician.' Rik shook his head,

and Grace liked that he wasn't arrogant enough to take charge.

'But I am,' she murmured.

Hurrying from the ballroom, down a plushly carpeted hall and then onto the polished granite floor of the main lobby, the concierge led them to the lifts, where a young waiter looked shell-shocked as he stood in the lift doorway, stopping the doors from closing.

Inside, a young woman was almost doubled over, each hand tightly gripping friends on either side of her.

'We didn't even know she was pregnant,' one of the women cried.

'We're supposed to be on a hen weekend,' the other added. 'She's getting married next week.'

'She's never even had the slightest bump,' the first woman chimed back in. 'I mean, a wedding dress was a bit tight at the last fitting and she was upset because she didn't know how she gained a few pounds. But that was about it.'

'Not a problem.' Grace shot them all a carefully crafted, soothing smile. 'I'm a doctor, I deal with babies every day and I'm here to help. Can I just get in there?'

The two friends looked at each other over the pregnant girl's head, apparently trying to decide which of them should go. It was evident that they both wanted to stay with their friend.

'Okay, you have two very good buddies here,'

Grace told the pregnant girl as she took control. Then she stepped into the side of the lift that had more room and gently disengaged one of the girls' hands, chivvying her out. 'Is there anyone you need to call?'

The friend shook her head, still resisting leaving the lift.

'Perhaps the groom?' Rik stepped up gently, steering the girl away as he shot Grace a meaningful look.

One that told her, without him even having to say a word, that she was free to concentrate on the case in hand, whilst he would deal with sorting everyone else out.

Whatever awkwardness had sprung up between her and Rik in that ballroom, it was dissipating quickly now. And for that, she was grateful.

'Oh, God, we never thought,' Grace heard the girl cry, flustered, as Rik led her away. 'He's my brother. I'll call him right now and tell him what's going on.'

'Good, great. We can sit in these chairs, where you can still see your friend. Shall I come with you?'

'Thanks.'

Briefly, Grace watched them leave, grateful for the way Rik stepped in so easily to handle that side of things. Then she turned her attention back to her patient.

'Okay, sweetheart, let's see what this baby is up

to, shall we? You're doing really well, and we're here with you now. I'm Grace, what's your name?'

'Her name's Emma,' the other friend answered for her.

'I didn't know.' The woman—Emma—gasped, a slick sheen of sweat covering her forehead and neck. 'I thought it was the stress of the wedding… that made me miss a few periods…'

She tailed off with a low moan as a contraction hit her. Grace waited until Emma was done.

'Well done, sweetheart. How far apart are the contractions?'

'I thought…they were period pains,' Emma began, puffing slightly. 'I thought it had come at last. I thought they would…ease off if we went shopping. I wasn't trying to hide it. I just…didn't know.'

'I understand,' Grace soothed. 'I'm not judging you, sweetheart. I just need to know how far apart your contractions are, and if you can walk.'

She looked out of the lift doors and across the shiny, dense granite of the lobby floor just as Emma shook her head emphatically.

'No. I…can't move.' She emitted a low cry.

Evidently, the contractions were very close. At least the inside of the lift had a somewhat more forgiving rubber floor.

'Not a problem, don't worry,' soothed Grace. 'I'm just going to take a look and see exactly where baby is up to, okay?'

'Okay.'

'Are you on any medication?'

'No.'

'The pill?'

'No, I came off it about a year ago.' Emma puffed, her breathing erratic and her words choppy as she fought past the waves of pain. 'We were supposed to get married six months ago but the wedding got postponed because of restrictions at the time. We...'

She let out a sharp sound, and Grace rubbed her hand over Emma's back.

'Take your time. You're doing brilliantly.

The mum-to-be offered a grateful, if exhausted smile.

'We were going to...try for a baby as soon as we were married.'

'That's good,' encouraged Grace. At least that meant they'd both wanted a baby. That would hopefully lessen the shock of the birth a little. 'Any history of disease or illness in the family?'

'Nothing,' Emma managed, after a moment.

After a few more questions and an examination, Grace was as confident as she could be that her patient was presenting without any additional, obvious complications. Emma was fully dilated and the baby was head-down and definitely coming. She craned her neck up to Rik, who was watching her even as he encouraged the rather flustered friend as she talked animatedly on her mobile phone.

'Rik, can you see where the ambulance crew is, and tell them we have a twenty-five-year-old female, prima-gravida, and that it's a precipitous birth,' she instructed him before turning swiftly back to her patient. 'It's okay, sweetheart. Everything is going to be okay.'

'Can we get her into a private room?' asked the hotel concierge.

Grace shook her head.

'I don't think we can risk it. She feels like pushing now so I think the best thing we can do is stay where we are. You could get some towels, clean water, and paper towels though.'

'I really don't think…'

'And maybe some gloves, too,' George told him firmly. 'That would be most helpful.'

Whatever objections he had to a woman giving birth in his hotel lift, he was going to have to set them aside. There was no way she was going to risk trying to move the mother-to-be when the birth was this imminent.

'Good girl, that's it. Keep trusting your body, you're doing really well.'

Then, as the concierge scurried off, muttering under his breath, and the young waiter was still holding the doors open, Grace crouched down ready to catch the baby if it fell.

In what felt like a few seconds later, Rik was

over with all the supplies she'd asked for, plus a large parasol from the garden restaurant.

'To afford our mum-to-be a little privacy,' he said simply. 'Now, what do you want me to do?'

'Thanks.' Grace couldn't help but like his consideration for her patient. 'What happened to the friend?'

'She's still talking to the groom—her brother—but I told the concierge to stay with her.' He dropped his voice a little lower so that only she could hear. 'I felt he was a little more interested in getting Emma out of his hotel lobby than in the fact that she was in labour.'

'Agreed,' Grace murmured in reply.

But whatever else she'd been going to say was cut off as Emma gave a deep grunt, which sounded to Grace as though she was bearing down. Another brief check, and Grace nodded.

'Okay, Emma, sweetheart, you're doing really well. On the next contraction, you give a push and we'll let gravity do the rest.'

'But my baby...'

'I'll catch baby, don't you worry.'

'Should she be lying down?' the remaining friend asked, worriedly.

'No, Emma's fine.' Grace offered a smile of assurance. 'In fact, standing up will help to facilitate the birth since it helps to widen the baby's pathway through the pelvis. That's it, Emma, you're doing well.'

Emma let out another primal grunt.

'Keep going, sweetheart, that's great. Your movement is an instinctive, age-old way to help humans manage the discomfort of labour. It's only in recent times that women have begun to give birth lying down.'

A few minutes later, it was all over. A flash of purple, and the baby came out like a rocket, straight into Grace's arms. Gratefully, she took the towel that Rik promptly offered her, and cleaned the baby.

'You're not cutting the cord?' he asked sharply.

'Not yet.' She continued attending to the baby. 'It gives time for some of the baby's blood to come back from their side of the placenta. Can be up to one hundred ccs.'

'That will make the blood quite a bit thicker,' he murmured.

'Yep, and it works as additional iron cells for the baby to help make red blood cells.'

'So how long do you wait?'

'I like to wait a few minutes, at least until the umbilical cord stops pulsing.' She smiled, as a loud cry rent the air.

'Good set of lungs.' Rik smiled at the half-smiling, half-sobbing new mum.

'It's a girl,' added Grace, finally cutting the cord and wrapping the baby up to hand to a still shocked Emma as she finished off. 'Ten perfect fingers and toes.'

She kept her voice upbeat, but Emma was still staring at the tiny, pink, shrivelled creature, as though she couldn't quite believe what had happened. Grace couldn't blame her, but before she could talk to the new mum, the concierge came bustling back over.

'The paramedics have just arrived,' he announced, with two cleaners in tow, and obvious relief.

Grace gritted her teeth.

'Great.' As she glanced over his shoulder to the crew hurrying in, her smile become more genuine. 'Over here, guys.'

They were colleagues she knew fairly well, and both of them shot her a brief greeting as they all crouched down around the new mum, and Grace began her handover.

'This is Emma, twenty-five. She has just given birth—less than ten minutes ago—to a baby daughter following a cryptic pregnancy. She had pseudo-bleeding, which she took to be light periods due to the stress of her upcoming marriage. The patient had no form of pain relief and there were no apparent complications during labour and delivery. There was no hormone injection to help the placenta to come out but, again, it hasn't even been ten minutes since delivery. She isn't on any medication and has no prenatal history. Mum and baby will need full assessment upon admission, and I recommend providing her, and her husband-to-be, with someone to talk to before they are discharged.'

'Thanks, Grace, we'll take it from here.' The paramedic shot her a rueful smile. 'You go back and enjoy what's left of your gala.'

'Thanks,' Grace replied, not bothering to tell them that she'd been leaving anyway.

They were more concerned with getting Emma and her newborn baby back to Thorncroft as quickly as possible. Still, Grace waited until the pair was safely loaded onto the ambulance, and it was on its way.

The concierge, having been blocked by Rik from rushing his cleaners in to clean up even around the poor ambulance crew's ankles, fired off a few snarky comments as he finally got his team to work.

'Thanks for your patience, guys,' Grace told the cleaners sincerely. She didn't miss their discreet eye-rolls of apology when the concierge's back was turned.

And as she made her way to the ladies' washroom to clean up, she heard Rik also offer a word of thanks. She couldn't stop herself from liking him all the more—not that it meant anything because by the time she'd finished tidying herself up, he would already be gone.

As he should be.

So why, when she emerged from the washroom

some time later, did her face feel as though it were going to crack with smiling when she saw Rik heading across the lobby towards her?

'Well.' He smiled that heart-stopping smile of his at her. 'That was a bit of unexpected drama.'

'It was,' she agreed as he cast her an amused look.

'One which I rather think you preferred to the gala.'

She wrinkled her nose.

'I did a bit, yes. And about the umbilical cord…'

'I wasn't criticising,' he assured her. 'Clearly you knew what you were doing back there. I was just curious. It's a long time since I did a training stint with Obstetrics.'

And what did it say that she liked his compliment as much as the fact that he was still so keen to learn new developments in other fields?

There was nothing worse than an arrogant surgeon, but Rik clearly wasn't one of them.

'Anyway—' she forced herself to speak '—I ought to leave.'

'How are you planning on getting home?'

Grace glanced around the lobby.

'I'll ask Reception to call a taxi for me.'

And then it was back—that strange undercurrent that ran between them. Only this time, there was something more substantial to it. As though their moment of working together with the birth had lent weight to their attraction.

Or perhaps she was reading into it because that was what she *wanted* to see.

Thrusting it aside, she headed to the desk.

'I'm so sorry, madam,' the receptionist apologised. 'There has been some kind of incident on the Metro, so all the taxis have been booked out for at least the next couple of hours. As a result, the hotel is keeping its restaurant open later, if you would like to dine with us.'

'No, that's okay.' Grace smiled, despite her suddenly pounding heart.

As if her body wasn't as unhappy as it ought to be at the idea of not being able to leave, after all.

'It's time I bought you that drink,' Rik announced abruptly.

And even though she knew she ought to decline, there wasn't a bit of her that seemed capable of doing so.

'That would be nice.' It was definitely her voice, but she hadn't intended to speak the words.

And as he led her across to the bar, she found her legs moving of their own free will. Apparently, both her body *and* mind were acting entirely independently of each other, God help her.

'Ahh, excuse me? Madam? If you please?'

Grace and Rik swung around as the concierge scuttled across the expanse of floor towards them.

'It seems our friend has found something else

to irk him,' Rik muttered quietly under his breath, making her stifle a laugh.

Almost as if she were some recalcitrant school-girl.

'You can't go in there.' The concierge slid himself between the two of them and the bar area.

'I believe we can.' Rik's tone might have been steady, and even, but disapproval seeped through nonetheless. 'And if you're going to address my companion here, I think I'd prefer you addressed her as *Doctor*, not *madam*.'

And Grace found it mirrored her own objections perfectly, even as the concierge twisted his face into a genteelly offended expression.

'You, sir, may of course go in, but I'm afraid your companion here may not.'

'I rather think we've earned it, no?' she added carefully.

'That's as may be.' He narrowed his eyes at them. 'But your dress is covered in blood, madam. I can't let you upset our other guests simply because you feel you deserve a drink.'

Grace halted abruptly, shame and humiliation slicing through her—emotions that she'd struggled to work out of her psyche for years. With Bas's help, she'd actually thought she'd overcome it. Which only made it all the more embarrassing now, that this man could make her feel so small.

'I…didn't realise,' she began apologetically. 'I just—'

'I believe what you're trying to say,' Rik cut in, his gaze firmly on the concierge, 'is that you're incredibly grateful for Dr Henley's intervention back there. Without her expert medical help, the situation with that young mother could have turned tragic.'

'However—' the concierge began, but Rik didn't allow him to continue.

'And, of course, *Dr* Henley wouldn't want to upset any of your other guests. Which is why, I imagine, you have another suggestion in mind. Especially as it appears we are being filmed.'

He jerked his head to the couple of mobile phones that were clearly pointed in their direction.

Grace edged self-consciously behind Rik, only too aware of the state of her attire.

The concierge, however, plastered a tight smile to his face.

'Of course, sir,' he noted with a polished air. 'The hotel would be only too happy to offer you the complimentary use of the Thistle Suite, complete with its own private entertaining area, where you and Dr Henley can enjoy your drink in peace.'

Grace nearly choked on swallowed air. The Thistle Suite in this place was famously one of the most coveted, and expensive, in the city. It was usually reserved for only the most exclusive VIP guests.

'Underbart.' Rik nodded his approval without

a trace of sarcasm, and Grace could only admire his style.

'Perhaps Dr Henley would also prefer a change of clothes, complimentary of course, from our hotel boutique?'

'That would be very kind,' Grace managed, hoping she could sound even a fraction as relaxed as Rik.

The concierge looked considerably happier.

'Very good. I'll take you up there now, and have the clothes sent along shortly. You can also send your dress for dry-cleaning, if you wish. I'm sure we can do something for those bloodstains. It is a designer dress, after all.'

'Thank you,' Grace managed again as they followed the man when he scurried across the floor to the reception desk.

'For the record,' she whispered to Rik, without knowing why it mattered to her, 'this dress might be designer, but I didn't buy it. I rented it.'

'I've heard about that.' He actually looked impressed and, despite her best efforts, Grace felt a sense of triumph. 'It's becoming something of a movement, is it not?'

'It is, and that's a good thing,' she agreed. 'But I've been doing it for years—ever since I was a med student with not a lot of money.'

'I don't think I attended many of these things when I was a student.'

'No.' She laughed. 'I wouldn't have normally.

But I have a friend who used to invite me to several galas, and other functions, each year, so that I could network—and so that I could throw his father off the scent when he inevitably snuck out of the party with some new female.'

'Nice of him,' Rik noted, though she couldn't help but think there was an odd tightness to his voice.

It was probably just her imagination.

'It was, actually. He had any number of contacts he could draw on, whilst I had none. He knew that and so he opened up his world to me. Without him I wouldn't be where I am now.'

Rik frowned.

'I'm sure that was your own talent, and hard work.'

'I'm not saying I didn't have to work hard.' She lifted her shoulders lightly, and then dropped them. 'Nor am I saying that I might not have got here eventually. But having those contacts made things easier. That's all.'

'This way, please.'

Obediently, Grace followed the man to the lifts, with Rik sauntering along in easy fashion, as though this happened to him every day.

Perhaps it did. He was certainly the sort of man for whom she imagined people jumping to attention.

By the time they reached the suite, Grace had just about managed to settle her jangling nerves.

And then the concierge opened the door, and the jangling reached a deafening level.

Nothing that she'd heard about the Thistle Suite could have prepared her for its sheer size. The footprint had to be about as big as the flat she'd worked so hard to buy and was so very proud of.

There were probably about as many rooms, too.

'It's just a series of spaces,' Rik whispered quietly.

She cast him a grateful smile. Clearly, he was somewhat accustomed to this kind of thing, which made her wonder quite how successful a plastic surgeon he had to be. Perhaps on the Jansens' level, after all.

Whilst here she was, struggling to pretend there wasn't some ridiculous thrill that ran though her at the idea of being in his hotel room.

'Go and get your shower,' Rik suggested. 'It's about three rooms away, but if you prefer, I can wait downstairs.'

She told herself that wasn't her heart kicking up another beat.

'Right. Lovely. Thank you.' She started through one door, before realising the bathroom was in the other direction. 'I'll be as quick as I can, and out of your hair as soon as possible.'

And she had to remind herself that it was just a turn of phrase when, in his low, rumbling voice, Rik told her to take her time.

CHAPTER FOUR

RIK WATCHED THE doorway for several minutes after Grace had left, trying to puzzle out what was going on.

He stared until some complimentary wine arrived, along with the fresh clothes for Grace. And then he glowered some more.

He'd spent his entire life keeping people at arm's distance—it was the safest way to handle them. And yet, from the moment he'd seen Grace Henley, that magnetic attraction had caught him off guard.

One dance with her and he'd felt greedy, and feverish, and a whole lot more when her firm, perfectly curved body had melded itself to his.

He felt strangely unbalanced, unable to remember when was the last time that any woman had managed to get under his skin quite like this. Had they ever? Either way, Rik only knew he wanted more. He wanted *her*. The hottest, hardest part of him did, anyway.

He sipped his wine, and wished it were something stronger. Richer. Something that would stop this inexplicable feeling of…jealousy…that seemed to be swirling around inside him.

He snorted to himself. He sounded drunk, yet he'd barely touched a drop. Perhaps it really was time to call it a night. He'd always been so tough. So unreachable. And yet…recently Rik thought he'd felt his famously ice-cool façade slipping. Ever since he'd found out who he really was and tracked down what remained of his so-called family.

As if finally achieving his goal of finding his brother had caused something to shift inside him. To…change.

Either way, there was no other way he would have let a woman, even one as captivating as Grace Henley, distract him from his main goal. Yet here he was.

Rik tried to shrug it off, but it was impossible.

For the better part of three decades, he'd stuffed down memories because they'd hurt too much to remember. It was odd, wasn't it, the things a person remembered? How the tiniest things could dislodge memories so deeply buried that one might have been forgiven for never knowing they existed.

Like playing schoolboy pranks, stealing pocketfuls of apples from Old Man's Nilsson's orchard, and sneaking out of their bedroom window at night to go and watch for the hedgehog family that had lived under the hawthorn hedge on the edge of the farmland.

How that wild, fun, free part of himself had died the moment he'd lost his beloved brother. How, the minute Bas had gone, it had felt to Rik as though the light had gone out in the entire universe.

He'd spent the better part of three decades mourning his bold, brave, full-of-life brother. He'd spent over twenty years actively searching for him. And he'd spent the past five months waiting for this very moment, when they would finally be reunited.

And now he was here—so close that he could practically taste it, like the finest, peatiest bourbon—he could feel the floodgates in his head being pushed and strained as he fought to hold back the slew of memories and emotions that were threatening to crash down on him at any moment.

It made Rik wonder if choosing the gala to approach Bas had been the best choice, after all. His intention had been neutral ground, outside the hospital where his brother—and he, as of Monday—worked.

But the closer the moment seemed to get, the more he was starting to wonder about why his brother hadn't replied to either of his previous letters. The thought that maybe Bas was deliberately ignoring him was finally began to gnaw into his brain. And the idea of it was almost too much to bear.

Three decades of missing his brother. Of imagining that glorious moment when they reunited.

He'd never once stopped to consider that Bas might not feel the same way.

That Bas...might not even have thought of his twin at all.

Something slithered through Rik. Something that felt like cold, hard rejection, all over again. But he didn't care to analyse it further. Bas *had* to want to see him. No other option was possible. And tonight was meant to have been their reunion.

Only his brother wasn't here.

But the mouth-watering Grace was.

The knock on the door came just as Grace was sliding her feet into the pretty flat pumps that had come with the clothing. She smoothed down the gorgeous steel-grey soft jersey trousers, and adjusted the short, floaty sleeves of the delicate cream top. As complimentary outfits went, it was surely the most expensive one the concierge could have chosen.

At last, she opened the door to the suite.

The time away had done little to diminish the impact of being face to face with Rik Magnusson.

'I didn't want to disturb you, but—' he apologised before stopping abruptly.

He stepped closer, and Grace realised she'd stopped breathing. And she couldn't seem to start again, no matter how hard she tried.

For what felt like an eternity—though logically

she knew was probably only a few seconds—she didn't dare to move as Rik's rich, disreputable eyes seemed to roam over her.

She felt ridiculously hot, and flustered. And molten.

Right *there*.

'You look stunning,' he told her, at length. But his eyes told her so much more. They whispered all the wicked thoughts that were already dancing around her head. Things she hadn't done before—not even in her dreams.

Disgracefully molten.

Grace smoothed down the jersey material again and tried to laugh it off—as though to prove she wasn't another of his adoring suitors.

'I don't think our concierge friend chose the clothes, do you?'

And if her voice was a little shaky, well, that could be her little secret.

'No?' Rik still seemed gratifyingly distracted.

'I rather suspect the boutique assistant did that,' she continued, if only to fill the silence. 'The outfit is too put-together, and he barely even wanted to help. Or maybe I'm being unfair on the man.'

'*Han var en pompös röv,*' Rik began hotly before correcting himself. 'He was a pompous ass.'

'Thank you.' She grinned.

'Reception have just called up to offer us a complimentary dinner on the house, and I wondered if you might like to get something to eat with me.'

'You don't need to do that. It's…' she checked her watch '…just after midnight. You could go to bed.'

Too late, she realised the folly of her suggestion. The last thing she needed was images of a semi-naked Rik in her head. Grace felt the familiar heat flushing through her and tried to beat it back.

She was more than a little grateful when Rik didn't appear to notice.

'And leave you sitting alone in the hotel lobby?' He quirked his eyebrows up. 'That wouldn't be particularly chivalrous, would it? So, will you dine with me?'

She hesitated, shoving all the uncharacteristically naughty thoughts out of her head. It *had* been several hours since she'd only picked nervously at a couple of elements of the sumptuous five-course gala meal. Even now, her stomach grumbled—its way of reminding her that the last time she'd eaten properly had probably been the day before.

Plus, she found that the offer of dining with this particular man was simply too good to pass up.

'If you're sure…' an odd grin tugged at the corners of her mouth, and it was all she could do to suppress it '…your company would be… very nice.'

Which didn't get anywhere close to articulating exactly what she thought spending a night in this man's company might be like.

Rather, she focussed on retrieving his key card for the suite before they left together, letting the door close behind them with what felt altogether too much like a click of finality.

As if her body wanted things that her brain would never allow itself to even contemplate.

'So,' Rik began as they made their way down the sumptuous hallway together. 'Tell me about Thorncroft.'

'Thorncroft,' she echoed, her brain struggling for a moment to right itself before reality plonked itself squarely on her chest.

So this was why he'd invited her to dinner. So that he could pump her for more information about the famous Jansen team—as outsiders tended to call it. She should have known.

'Which one do you want to hear about first?' Somehow she dredged up a smile.

'Which one?' he echoed neutrally.

He played it well, but she wasn't a fool.

'Magnus? Or Bas?'

'Neither,' Rik replied.

And, as daft as it seemed, for a moment she was almost convinced that he'd surprised even himself.

'Don't be silly, I'm not offended.' She pasted on another bright expression. 'Everyone wants to know about Magnus and Bas Jansen. Even new colleagues who aren't on the surgical exchange programme.'

'And yet, what I want to know most is what brought you to Thorncroft.'

'Me?'

'You,' he confirmed. 'Dr Grace Henley. Tell me your story, *älskling*. I find I want to hear it all.'

And even though a part of her desperately wanted to believe he was interested, her more sceptical side tried to remind herself to be on her guard for him using her to get inside information on Magnus and Bas.

This wasn't at all the way he'd intended his evening to go when he'd first decided to fly to the UK early, in order to attend the Jansen medical ball.

But he couldn't seem to regret a moment of it—not when he was spending it in the company of this woman. Yet, none of this made sense.

He wasn't like the playboy brother he'd travelled all this way to meet again. He didn't pick women up in bars—or at galas, if he was going to be technical—and take them home for one night of wild abandon. He wasn't a monk, of course, but he picked his companions carefully.

Always professional women who were as career-minded as he was, so who wouldn't want more from him than he was prepared to give. Attractive, too, admittedly. There had to be some chemistry.

Though never like this. Never so strong that he'd had to physically remove himself from the suite upstairs, lest he draw her into the bedroom and tear off all those new clothes that she kept subconsciously skimming down over a body he could already tell was nothing less than luscious.

Because she wanted him, just as badly. He knew women well enough to read her dilated pupils, her erratic pulse, and the way she responded to him. Just as he'd read the way her body had moulded itself so exquisitely to his when they'd been dancing earlier.

They might well have passed one perfect lifetime just spinning around that floor together. And Rik could easily imagine passing several more lifetimes doing the same.

He could pretend that he'd only brought her here to try to find out a little more about his brother, and his father, but Rik knew it would have been a lie. Despite his questions about Thorncroft, she'd seemed wary, almost cagey in her replies, and in a way he hadn't cared.

Given the choice between plugging her for information about his long-lost family, and spending more time just enjoying her company, he'd known exactly what he preferred.

'Another coffee?' he asked as she replaced the delicate cup back on the saucer.

Anything to prolong the meal, and their time together. *What had got into him?*

She tipped her head from one side to the other, ruefully, and the soft blonde bun—a 'messy' bun, he had once heard it called—tilted with her.

He wanted to know what that would look like down, cascading over her bare, elegant shoulders.

'I shouldn't have had that one really,' she answered with mock sorrow. 'I'll never sleep tonight.'

He bit back the suggestions in his head, and he knew it wasn't just his imagination when she plastered on an over-bright smile.

'I guess I really ought to see if there are any taxis available by now.'

'Of course.' It shouldn't have been a struggle for him to sound gentlemanly. 'We'll go and speak to the front desk.'

He stood, letting her step out in front of him; her blue eyes were just as bright when they met his. Then he placed his hand at the small of her back to guide her and, without a word, she seemed to melt into him, and Rik knew there was no fighting it any longer. Not for either of them.

Without a word, they left the still-busy restaurant together, heading across the lobby and towards the bank of lifts rather than the reception post.

It was only when they were inside, the metal doors sliding closed in front of them, that Rik turned her to face him, pulling her in, as she looped her arms around his neck.

'You're quite sure, *älskling*?' Rik's voice was gruff, and needy. And he watched with satisfaction—and not a small degree of triumph—when it raked over her, leaving her skin goosebumping with desire.

'Do I look unsure?' she challenged, inching that fraction closer to him.

He wondered if Grace had any idea of *how* she looked. Breathless, dizzy, and charged with adrenalin. She was every last schoolboy fantasy he'd ever had, and more. So much more.

But she still didn't really answer his question until she reached up onto her toes, pushed her face closer to his, and pressed her lips to his.

And he felt astoundingly reckless.

It was not a feeling he was accustomed to, having spent his entire adult life—and much of his childhood one—being the voice of reason. Grounding his alternatively self-aggrandising then self-sabotaging mother. Caring for her when she pushed everyone else away with her temper and her cruelty.

As if it had been his penance.

But now, he felt as though this—Grace—was somehow his reward for all of those years.

She made him feel…free. Alive. As though life was finally meant for living.

At least, that was what Rik told himself as he

pressed her back against the wall of the lift. His mouth plundering hers, over and over, as if he couldn't get enough of her taste. As if he'd been waiting for her his entire life.

That alone should have been enough to make him stop—this *thing* wasn't why he'd worked so hard, and sacrificed so much, to get where he was—but instead, the only thing it did was spur him on.

It felt too *right*.

Rik had no idea how they managed to draw apart, moments before the lift doors slid smoothly open at his floor. Nor how they made it down the infernally long, deserted corridor to his room. But as soon as the key card was activated, he found himself hauling her back to him as they tumbled through the door.

It wasn't enough.

He wanted more. To touch her, to taste her, to make her his—especially when she opened her mouth to his tongue and rolled her hips against the hardest part of him. As if she wanted all that, too.

Rik wasn't sure how long they stayed there, against the hotel-room door, kissing like a couple of passionate teenagers. It could have been a lifetime. Longer. But when he hoisted her up into his arms, with Grace wrapping her legs around his hips as though she'd been specially crafted just for him, he found he didn't want to wait any longer.

Carrying her across the room and depositing her on the luxurious bed, he made short work of divesting her of those clothes that had been a symphony to every last, glorious curve.

'Härlig...' he breathed. 'You are stunning, *älskling.* I want to taste every inch of you.'

'Show me,' his vision whispered huskily.

Rik needed no further invitation.

An instant later, his own clothes had followed hers onto the floor of the suite, and his body was moving deliciously slickly over hers, as if they'd been waiting for this moment all night.

'Rik...' she breathed, shifting beneath him, the softest, hottest, wettest part of her skimming his as though she was ready for him.

If he didn't move now and slow it down, he wasn't sure that he wouldn't embarrass himself. He wanted her so badly that his body actually physically hurt. It would have been so easy to take what she was offering to him.

But he wanted so much more than that. For both of them.

So instead, he silenced her by dipping his head to the sensitive hollow at the base of her neck, and kissing her whilst she sighed and let her hands explore their way up his biceps and to his shoulder muscles. As if learning his body, the way he intended to learn hers.

All night, if he had to.

Slowly, with a leisureliness that almost killed him, Rik acquainted himself with every curve, every line, every ridge of this magnificent creature. He explored one side of her collarbone, then the other, delighting in the shivers that ran through her body as she arched this way, then that, in response.

Then, he trailed his kisses across the tempting swell of her chest, drawling whorls with his tongue before reaching one perfect, pink-nippled breast, and lavishing it with attention that had Grace writhing sweetly beneath him.

He used his fingers, his tongue, even the faintest hint of his teeth, as he licked, and played, and teased. And when she cried out his name again, her hands raking over his back, he simply turned his attention to the other side, and played some more.

Rik lost all sense of time. There was only Grace, and him, and the long night stretching complicitly out before them.

He made his way from one side of her incredible body to the other, using scorching-hot kisses and teasing patterns with his tongue. He blazed a trail downwards to her lower abdomen, then dropped to halfway up the inside of her thighs where he took his time working his way upwards. Until finally, *finally* he was *there*. Where he most ached to taste her.

And then, he made himself slow down even further.

It was like some kind of exquisite torture, lifting his head to instead let his hand wander over the sensitive skin at the top of her legs. Revelling in the way her hips rolled for him as he moved from one side to the other, doing nothing more than deliberately skimming her wet heat with his knuckles. The sound of his name on her lips possibly the sexiest thing he thought he'd ever heard.

As if her sweet scent weren't driving him almost crazy with need.

Finally, when he didn't think either of them could take it any more, he dropped his head between her legs and licked straight into her core.

And, Lord, her luscious, honeyed taste was even better than he'd been dreaming of. He couldn't get enough. Again and again he tasted her, teased her, feeling that heavenly pressure build up in her as her hips moved and her body danced that dance of old.

'Rik...' she murmured, half a question.

But he could tell everything that he needed to from her taste, and he simply slid his hands under her perfect backside, growling into her until she shivered with need. Until she slid her fingers into his hair and began to writhe against his mouth.

And then he licked her some more. The sound of her moans—thicker and faster now—and his name on her breath making his body tighter than he thought it had ever, ever been. As if no woman had ever counted before her.

He could feel the tension building in her, banking hotter, and higher, until suddenly he knew she was close to the edge, bucking against him as she half gasped, and half cried. And then Rik slid his finger inside her as he sucked on the very centre of her need. Hard, and long, as she screamed out his name and shattered around him.

The most perfect sound he thought he'd ever heard.

By the time Grace came back to herself, feeling more torn apart, yet more whole than she thought she'd ever felt, Rik was already moving his body over her. The feel of his solid, muscled body making her ache to touch him more.

To offer him the same flawless high that he'd just given her.

Dimly, in the furthest reaches of her brain, it occurred to her that—from this moment—she was ruined for any other man. No other encounter she'd ever had—not that there had been many—had even come close to this. She suspected no man in the future ever would.

But she didn't care. Because if this was the best she would ever have the fortune to experience, then she was damned well going to revel in every single, last moment of it.

'That was…' she began, hoping he couldn't hear the slight shake in her laugh.

The one that revealed how come-apart she still felt.

'Only the beginning,' Rik cut in, dipping his head to kiss her throat, her neck, and that sensitive hollow below her ear.

She sighed with pleasure, even as she shifted beneath him. And then, suddenly, he was between her legs. His hard, dizzying maleness nestled right against where she was still molten and soft. Making her want, *need*, all over again.

And it was only then that an alarm started to sound in her head. Dim. Muffled. But there, all the same.

She paused, her mind floundering as she tried to work out what the ringing was. And then it struck her.

How could she possibly have forgotten? *She*, of all people.

'Wait,' she muttered, pushing herself upright from beneath him, though she had no idea how she had the strength to do so. 'Do you have… protection?'

'Protection?' He looked at her for a moment—stunned.

It occurred to Grace that it was more than a little flattering to realise that Rik had been as caught up in the moment as she'd been. That, like her, he'd almost forgotten himself.

'I think they have something in the minibar,' he managed grimly, after a moment.

Yes, now that he mentioned it, she thought she'd heard that, too. She nodded jerkily.

'Intimacy kits.' Her tongue felt thick in her mouth, and she hated that the moment had become so awkward.

'Shall I?' Rik asked, moving across the room with no hint of embarrassment as her eyes traced his magnificent naked form.

He was asking her if she wanted to continue. Making sure her hesitation was simply a matter of practicality, and that she hadn't changed her mind.

What did it say about her that his consideration felt like the most romantic thing anyone had ever done for her?

'Yes,' she managed thickly. But with certainty.

And she watched as Rik obliged, retrieving the kit and removing a condom with an efficiency of movement that helped to erase any awkwardness between them. And then he was heading across the room, taking a moment to roll it on in a way that made her breath catch in her throat, before slipping back between her legs as though nothing had happened at all.

Making her feel at ease, all over again.

Bending her knees up, Grace let her hands glide down his hewn, muscled back, and arched up to him.

'There's no rush,' he murmured.

But it was the tight edge to his voice that thrilled her the most. As if he was barely restraining himself. As if he wanted her too badly.

'You call this rushing?' she complained on uneven breaths even as the corners of her mouth turned upwards. 'Glaciers move quicker.'

'You're taunting me.' His eyes darkened. Rich and delicious.

'I am,' she agreed, her voice still choppy.

'Is that so, *älskling*?' His intent eyes darkened to almost black. His tone deceptively even. 'Because, trust me, that cuts both ways.'

It could have been a threat or a promise—most likely it was both. A thrill rippled through Grace. She might have tried to start this little game of dares, but she had a feeling he planned on winning it.

'Suit yourself,' she retorted deliberately. Her pulse speeding up as he trailed a finger down her body.

If he wanted to win, that was fine by her. In fact, anything was fine by her so long as...

She gasped with pleasure as Rik thrust into her. Slick, and slow, and deep.

He was big, stretching her everywhere. Making parts of her *feel* things where she didn't think she ever had before. Not that she'd ever thought her previous boyfriends had been *bad* at sex. They just hadn't been as good as *this*.

As intense, and incredible, and breath-stealing as being with Rik felt like.

And then he began to move, and every other thought fled her brain. There was only this. Only now.

He slid out, then in. Out. In. All the while his gaze was holding hers, his mesmerising eyes reflecting back that same raw hunger that coursed through her very veins. The entire world fell away as Grace gave herself up to this captivating man.

Again.

Stroke after stroke, he built the fire inside her. And all she could do was cling on. Wrapping her arms, her legs, right around him, and letting him take them wherever he pleased—their breath intermingling, drawing them closer together.

Rik began to move faster now. Harder. Each slick thrust propelling her on to a new high. She didn't know how she broke the eye contact. She only knew that she needed to lift her head so that she could press her lips against his neck. She had to taste the faint, glorious tang of salt with her tongue. To graze his skin with her teeth.

He groaned—a low sound that seemed to rumble right through her, and to her very core—and plunged in harder. Grace gasped, lifting her hips to meet him, revelling in the faster rhythm. Matching him, thrust for thrust.

And then she felt that wave building above her, ready to crash over and tear her apart. She was ready for it. She needed it. Raking her hands down his back, she arched her body, and he did something magical, and she was lost. Completely and perfectly.

Crying out his name as she soared into blissful nothingness.

And the last thing she remembered was Rik calling out her name, too, as he soared right along with her.

CHAPTER FIVE

'GOOD MORNING.' RIK glanced around the teaching hospital's Jansen Auditorium—yet another reminder of his father and brother's power. 'My name is Rik Magnusson and I'm here as part of the Jansen Exchange Programme,'

Why invite unwanted gossip by introducing himself by any other name?

He glanced around the audience again, not particularly surprised that neither of them was present. He didn't even feel disappointed. It was only what he'd expected.

What had caught him off-guard, however, was that he also found himself looking for Grace in the audience.

Grace, the woman who had shared his bed for the weekend. The woman who was supposed to have been nothing more than an unanticipated yet pleasant diversion from the disappointment of not seeing his brother at the Jansen Gala.

Yet now he was searching for her. Eager to see her. Rik didn't care to examine what that said about him. All he knew was that being here, in the UK, a stone's throw from his long-lost brother, was playing with his head.

It was making him feel...odd things. He couldn't explain it exactly, but it was making him want to share his reasons for being at Thorncroft with this woman. He—who had never told a single soul about his childhood, or his twin brother.

So instead, he yanked his wayward thoughts back into line, opting to engage with the group of doctors and surgeons who would be his colleagues for the next three months.

'But you guys aren't interested in why I'm here, are you?' He smiled, moving away from the podium and walking across the floor. 'You want to know about the case I've brought with me. So, let's get started.'

A low rumble of laughter ran around the room, and Rik started the programme on his laptop, perched on the side table, and watched the images flash onto the main screen on the stage.

This was what he did best—the medical side. Not the emotional.

'This is Kenny, a nine-year-old boy who presented with occult craniosynostosis.'

Another rumble went around the room. This time of interest, rather than laughter.

'Craniosynostosis, as I'm sure most of you know, is the premature fusion of cranial sutures—otherwise known as the fibrous joints—between the skull bones,' Rik continued, conversationally. 'Would any of the junior house officers care to tell me what makes this case particularly interesting? Yes, you. Go ahead.'

'Craniosynostosis occurs in approximately one

in every two thousand live births,' the young doctor Rik had selected sat up in his seat confidently. 'It's usually diagnosed and treated within the first year of life, though.'

'Good.' Rik nodded. 'Delayed diagnosis craniosynostosis beyond those first twelve months is uncommon. However, as you can see from this photo, our patient presents as a relatively normocephalic nine-year-old. He displays none of the normal head-shape anomalies or syndromic diagnosis which would usually have alerted a paediatrician to potential craniosynostosis, earlier in infancy.'

Rik stopped, his attention broken as the door at the top of the room opened unexpectedly. It wasn't loud enough to distract the audience, not least since it was behind them and they were all still assessing the images on the large screen. But despite every part of his brain roaring at him to ignore it, instinct made Rik look.

Grace. Somehow, he'd known it was her even before she'd stepped into view.

His eyes tracked her movements as she walked down a couple of steps, then a couple more, before stopping abruptly and sliding elegantly into an end seat.

Suddenly, it was as though her presence—her interest—made him feel taller. Lighter.

Ridiculous.

And yet, as she settled in one of the seats near

the top, it cost him far more than it ought to have done to drag his attention back to his presentation.

'The patient presented with increasingly debilitating migraines, optic nerve oedema, and issues consistent with ICP—increased intercranial pressure, which was confirmed by invasive monitoring. Additionally, CT scan showed pan-suture craniosynostosis. Initial questions?'

'Is there any family history of craniosynostosis?' called out one voice.

'There is not,' Rik confirmed.

'What about a family history of migraines?' another voice added after a moment.

'Good. Yes.' Rik nodded. 'The patient's biological father has always suffered with debilitating migraines, but, again, had never been diagnosed with any craniofacial abnormalities.'

'So, then, you're recommending cranial vault remodelling?' asked one doctor.

'Obviously he is, or we wouldn't be here,' another joked.

Still, Rik liked the way the original speaker didn't back down.

'My point is, given that the father may have dealt with occult craniosynostosis all his life, and also given the debate surrounding the functional benefits of cranial remodelling, I was simply wondering how you came to the conclusion that surgery was the right option in this case, Dr Magnusson?'

'It's a good question,' Rik agreed, 'and one which I find important. Any thoughts?'

A lively debate sprang up between those cautioning against surgery when there was no clear need, and those who thought it was worth trying to see if it could alleviate the issue.

And then Grace spoke out.

'I would want to know what the impact has been on the patient's life. Most notably, the migraines and his ability to lead a normal life.'

Rik dipped his head in agreement. It might not be her field, but it didn't surprise him how quickly she got to the crux of the issue.

'According to the family, the migraines began as headaches that have become increasingly debilitating over the past couple of years.'

'He's nine,' Grace mused, her eyes locked with his. 'So what about his schooling? Has it been affected?'

There might as well have been no one else in the room. He could see only her.

'The patient's migraines have resulted in a significant number of days absent from school,' confirmed Rik. 'His family have noted increasing difficulty in learning, and there are issues concerning the patient's temper along with an increasing number of violent outbursts—most likely as a result of the pain—which have led to our nine-year-old being expelled from school.'

'In that case,' she noted, those green-blue

depths still fixed with his, 'I would agree that surgical intervention looks to be the most beneficial treatment. Whilst the patient may not need cranial vault remodelling to rectify any craniofacial abnormalities, the procedure would nonetheless create a space into which the brain could expand.'

'That could help to alleviate the migraines, and the optic oedema as mentioned before,' another voice noted thoughtfully.

'Which was the conclusion I came to,' Rik confirmed.

But it took more effort than it should have done for him to drag his eyes from Grace and remember to address the rest of the group.

Every second of their weekend together was burned, so insanely brightly, into his brain. If he closed his eyes, he was certain he could still see her, smell her, *taste* her. He still wanted her with a feverishness that he couldn't explain. It made him physically ache. Worse, it made something ache deep inside his chest.

Incredibly, no one else appeared to have noticed anything amiss.

So much for his 'stone-cold' reputation. All he had seemed to feel, since that moment at the gala, was fire.

And molten heat.

Rik had no idea how he concluded his lecture but finally, finally, they were wrapping up and he was accepting words of thanks, and offers to assist in Theatre, as the group filed out of the lecture room.

And then it was just him and Grace alone in the vast space, and common sense tapping valiantly against his brain.

This couldn't happen.

'Good lecture,' she complimented as he busied himself disconnecting the laptop from the system and shutting it down. 'You had them eating out of the palm of your hand.'

'It's an interesting case.'

He was deflecting, but it was either that or haul her back into his arms to take up where they'd left off.

Back where she belongs, a strange, uninvited voice whispered.

He silenced it.

Maybe there was still an unspent attraction between them, and maybe they could explore it during the course of the next couple of months. But not yet. Not until he'd found his brother and had the conversation that was decades overdue.

He could tell himself it was because he always put the priority tasks ahead of pleasure, and that he'd come here to find his brother long before he'd laid eyes on this woman. And perhaps there would even be a degree of truth in it.

But it wasn't the entire reason.

The truth was more along the lines of the fact

that he hated lying to her. Or, more accurately, avoiding telling her the truth.

How many times, this past weekend, had she asked him about himself only for him to have to divert the conversation simply because he hadn't been able to answer her the way a part of him had wanted to do?

He was renowned for playing his cards close to his chest, yet even from that first night he'd wanted to tell this woman the secrets that he'd never told anyone else.

He hadn't, of course. Because that would have been illogical. And he was all about sense, and rationale.

And rationally, Rik knew acting out of character had to be down to finally being in contact with his brother, after decades of searching. It was understandable that being so close after all this time had stirred emotions within him whether he'd intended it to, or not.

That didn't mean he had to share his innermost thoughts with some stranger. Besides, it wasn't just his secret to share.

The sooner he tracked his elusive brother down and finally spoke with him, the better.

Grace had always thought of herself as a normal woman. Perhaps a little quiet at times, and something of a wallflower at parties, and she'd never had a one-night stand before. She was committed to her career far more than she was committed to a relationship, though she couldn't call herself a nun, or even a virgin.

That one night when she'd been sixteen had seen to that.

But then she'd gone to that ball before the weekend where she'd met Rik, and all those hitherto ridiculous books and films about *wanting* and *lusting* meant nothing when held up against this tumultuous, febrile *yearning* that seemed to tumble and roll underneath every inch of her very skin.

This *aching* that was almost too much to bear.

It was the reason she'd been unable to keep away from his lecture. Not simply because she'd been interested in the case he was bringing to Thorncroft, but because she'd actually itched to see him again.

So much for her immunity to men. She'd found herself in the corridor outside the lecture theatre before she had even realised she'd been drawn there.

The next thing she'd known, she'd been opening the door and creeping inside. When he'd looked up to see her walking down the steps, she'd almost forgotten anyone else had been in there, and so very nearly kept moving all the way down to the bottom, and onto that stage in front of him.

And now, she was here, having waited for everyone else to leave. As though he would have wanted her to stay behind. As though he saw her as anything other than the extended one-night stand that she knew she'd been.

If she didn't want to look desperate, then she needed to pull things back to a more professional footing.

'You didn't mention that you were one of the foremost authorities on craniosynostosis,' she countered.

'I seem to recall that we didn't do a lot of talking,' he drawled, and she felt herself flush—the stain creeping down her neck and beneath the neckline of her top.

And it only made it all the hotter when his eyes watched every inch of its journey. She tried to speak but couldn't.

'Do you have a particular interest in this area of medicine?' Rik asked at length, rescuing her.

She bobbed her head a little over-eagerly.

'I have a case of a two-month-old, which I think may be craniosynostosis.'

That much, at least, was true.

'My speciality is delayed diagnosis of craniosynostosis,' Rik pointed out. 'Usually in pre-adolescence, and adolescence. Not in babies.'

'I understand that,' she acknowledged lightly. 'But you must have carried out multiple surgeries on babies diagnosed within the first year of life, before you specialised in delayed diagnosis craniosynostoses?'

'I have,' he admitted, though she got the sense he hadn't meant to.

It gave her a certain kind of hope, and she wasn't sure how she refrained from reaching up and pressing her lips to his. Just to see if he tasted as good as she remembered.

'Is the family in the hospital now?'

Grace shook her head.

'I have the case notes, though. Although you'll have to brace yourself—the main part of Thorncroft Royal Infirmary is nowhere near as luxurious as the Jansen wing.'

'That's hardly surprising,' Rik remarked dryly. 'I have to say that, although I had heard the Jansen clinic was a top-spec facility, I wasn't prepared for quite how luxurious it is. Even the damned coffee machines in this wing are espresso machines that wouldn't look out of place in a high-class coffee house in town. Complete with barista.'

Grace grinned.

'Everything in this place is top of the range,' she confirmed. 'From the marble floors to the latest light fittings in the bathrooms. There are even two helipads on the roof, one for emergencies and the other for VIP clients.'

'Of course it is.' Rik exhaled. 'And what about the building annexed to the hospital? The low-rise vertical garden apartment building?'

Grace was surprised.

'That's the one I was telling you about the night of the gala.' She flushed suddenly, but pressed on. 'It belongs exclusively to the Jansen wing. The lower floors are dedicated rehab areas, luxury pools, and spas, and gyms, and the upper levels are given over to VIP patients and/or their entourages.'

'So it's basically a luxury hotel for patients and their stylists, PR, make-up?'

'Not just them.' Grace refused to take the bait. 'The mid-levels are for visiting consultants. That's where you would have been put up had you not opted for The Marham.'

'I asked to be put up in a hotel,' he corrected swiftly. 'I never said it needed to be as luxurious as The Marham.'

'You wanted a bolt-hole away from the hospital?' she guessed.

It was something she probably would have wanted, too. She loved working at Thorncroft, but it was also nice just to be able to go home.

Which brought her right back to her recent hankering for a complete change of scene.

'I knew the Jansen clinics catered to celebrity clients,' Rik noted. 'But I didn't realise quite the scale.'

No, she didn't suppose he did. That was the art of what Magnus and Bas achieved—however much they differed on the means—in medical arenas, the Jansen name was more synonymous with pushing the boundaries of their field.

'Magnus makes the Jansen facilities their money by carrying out some of the best elective procedures in the country, and to do that he needs to attract the elite. Bas used that income to push the boundaries of reconstructive surgery from some of the neediest patients worldwide.'

'So effectively, Bas gives the Jansen name its medical kudos, whilst Magnus makes enough money that it would make your eyes water?'

'I suppose you could put it like that,' though it sounded a little harsh. 'Also, as far as those vertical gardens go, Magnus wanted one of the most acclaimed British architects to design the apartment complex, whilst Bas insisted it should be environmentally friendly. Eventually, they agreed that a leading botanist of Bas's choosing would work with the architect Magnus wanted.'

Rik arched his eyebrows tellingly.

'I can't deny that the result is incredible. It looks as if a lush, green, leafy park has met the most cutting-edge building.'

That was exactly what it was; Grace nodded.

'All part of the Jansen brand,' he remarked dryly. 'I see that you're setting the bar extremely high for me.'

And she liked quite how self-effacing he was. In fact, it turned out, she liked an awful lot about Rik Magnusson.

'By all accounts, you've already set the bar high for yourself.' She flushed. 'Obvious, I guess, since you wouldn't have been selected for the exchange programme if you hadn't, but you have to know that the craniosynostosis you just presented is going to be the talk of the hospital.'

He eyed her for a moment.

'If it interests you, put your name forward to work on the surgery with me.'

She started, surprised.

'I'm Obstetrics. I'm not Plastics.'

'Nor are half the doctors who were just in that room, and you had plenty of good suggestions— you weren't exactly a lurker. Besides, isn't this hospital supposed to be about teaching?'

She chewed her lip thoughtfully. The idea was tempting, but she couldn't decide if he was suggesting it because he truly felt she would benefit from it, or simply because they'd had sex—and he wanted more.

And you don't? A wry voice crept into her head.

She shut it down—just as Rik started speaking again.

'Okay, so I have another meeting to get to now, but perhaps we could meet tonight for dinner? Say half-past seven?'

She was sure she forgot how to breathe—if only for a moment.

Crazy.

'Dinner sounds lovely.' She wasn't sure how

she succeeded in sounding so composed. 'But it won't let you see my case files on my patient.'

'I see.' His lips twitched. And she had the insane urge to kiss them into submission. 'Then how about we meet around lunchtime in the coffee shop I saw downstairs?'

'Julian's?' Grace clarified. 'All right. Shall we say around half-twelve?'

Rik took out his mobile.

'Give me your number in case either of us get held up.'

'At lunchtime?' she verified, before she could stop herself.

'At lunchtime for the case. And also tonight, at dinner.'

Lord, he was too perfect.

'Right, fine. Good.' She blinked at him as he eyed her steadily, his fingers on the buttons of his phone as he waited for her details. But she couldn't think. Her mind had gone completely blank. 'Wait...may I?'

Taking his phone, she drew in a steadying breath as she took a moment to fire her brain back into action. Then, punching in her digits quickly, she handed it back to him.

Within moments, he'd texted her a silly face, which made her grin inanely.

'I should get back to the ward, but I'll see you then.' She spun around and hurried out of the room, leaving him in her wake.

Before she did anything foolish, as much as because her morning of scans was about to begin.

She really shouldn't feel so giddy. Grace lifted her fingers tentatively to her still-grinning face as she hurried along the corridor.

But surely she could bask in it for a few more moments—when did this kind of thing ever usually happen to her?

When had she ever let it? That one mistake as a sixteen-year-old had been enough to frighten her off acting on impulse for good. Not least when it came to men.

But then, she'd never met any man quite like Rik before.

CHAPTER SIX

'HOW ARE YOU DOING?'

Grace stepped into the scrub room, where Bas was cleaning up after one of his surgeries.

'The surgery went well,' he acknowledged, his tone neutral.

Grace tried not to grimace. This was so like Bas, to shut people out. Though not usually her.

Still she pressed on.

'I didn't mean the surgery. I meant you.'

For a moment, she wasn't sure he was going to answer. He sluiced his arms side to side under the water.

Left.

Right.

Left.

Right.

Grace waited, unsure what to say. Something had...shifted between them recently. It had started a few months before.

He'd received a letter: he'd thought she hadn't seen it, but she had. One morning, it had been sitting on the desk in his opulent office in the Jansen wing. By the time she'd visited in the afternoon, the letter had been in the bin. Unopened.

And he'd started to shut down from there. Little by little.

It was one of the reasons that she'd held off from telling him that she was thinking about leaving Thorncroft. That, and the fact that a part of her was scared to make such a big move.

But it hadn't stopped the niggling voice inside her from growing louder. Telling her that this wasn't the place for her any more.

Had it not been for Naomi's scan the night of the gala, she would have told Bas then. It had been her plan. But then there had been Naomi. And then she'd met Rik. And everything seemed to have drifted between her and Bas.

Would he shut Naomi out the same way? She couldn't help but wonder. Bas's deep voice pulled her back to the present.

'You mean, aside from the fact that my unborn baby is going to need surgery mere days after she's born?'

'I'm so sorry,' Grace told him sincerely. 'I can only imagine what you and Naomi are going through.'

'Thanks.' His voice sounded almost unfamiliar to her. It took her a moment to realise that it was emotion. 'No amniocentesis results?'

'Not yet.' She frowned. 'Seddon put a rush on it, but it still takes time—you know that.'

His only response was one of his trademark grunts. She dreaded to think what was running through his head.

'Do you and Naomi know what you're going

to do yet?' she asked. 'In terms of raising the baby, I mean?'

He cast her a dark look.

'Do you mean how involved am I going to be? It's my child, Grace. Or do you think the same as Naomi? Namely that I'll just *dip in and out of their lives*?'

Ah, was that what was bothering him?

'Is that what Naomi thinks? That you wouldn't be dependable?' Grace asked gently. She could see how that would get under Bas's skin. But she could see Naomi's point of view, too. 'Then again, she doesn't know you. You hide the real you well, so I guess you can see her side of it, can't you?'

'Not really,' he bit out. 'She asked me what you meant when you talked about me not being like Magnus. Or my mother.'

Grace didn't answer straight away. If she'd known Naomi could overhear the telephone conversation then she might have been a little more guarded. Yet perhaps it was no bad thing for Bas to be forced to open up to this woman a little more. After all, Naomi was carrying Bas's baby. For better or worse, the two of them were going to be part of each other's lives for ever, surely the poor woman deserved to know a little more about the father of her unborn child.

She doubted Naomi had deliberately set about getting pregnant by Bas—though many a woman had certainly tried. But there was something about the other woman that Grace had instantly liked. She got the impression that random hook-ups were about as common an occurrence in Naomi's life as they were in her own.

Or had been, until the other night, Grace thought abruptly as a sinful image of Rik filled her mind.

She shoved it away hastily and blew out a breath.

'You didn't answer, did you?'

'I don't see that it's any of her business.'

She almost felt sorry for her friend. *Almost*.

'You can hear the absurdity of your comment, right?' Grace prodded softly. 'Naomi is the mother of your unborn child. Like it or not, she has a right to hear a little about your past, and the way it shaped you.'

'Does she?' countered Bas. 'It isn't as though we've chosen to be together. If it weren't for this pregnancy, we probably wouldn't have even spoken again.'

If it hadn't been for that odd shadow that skittered across his features, she might have believed him.

'Wouldn't you?' she asked, carefully.

'What's that supposed to mean?'

Grace wrinkled her nose, trying to choose her words carefully.

'It means that I don't think I've ever seen you act quite the way you did around Naomi. And it isn't just that she's pregnant, or that you were both dealing with the news that no parent-to-be wants to hear, because I noticed even before the scan.'

'You're imagining things,' Bas countered scornfully.

But Grace couldn't help feeling it lacked any real emphasis. As if he was just playing a part.

But to fool other people—or himself?

'I don't think so. There was just something… different, about the way you were around her. The softer side of Bas that I usually only see when you and I are alone. I think you like her, Bas. And I think you think so, too.'

He glowered at her for a moment then, tellingly, abruptly changed the topic.

'How did the gala go?' he demanded, stepping off the foot tap and drying his hands.

Grace paused. She'd wanted to say more about him and Naomi, but it didn't seem like the right moment.

Not least when thoughts of Rik were now suddenly tearing around her head.

'The gala went very smoothly,' she assured him. 'People asked after you, naturally, but I just said you were caught up in a case here. In any case, a record amount of money was raised, and a good night was had by all.'

Guilt chased through her and, as if he could tell, Bas's voice sounded slightly sharper than usual.

'Nothing else to tell?'

Or perhaps it was simply her imagination. She eyed him warily.

'Are you talking about the new doctor on your exchange programme?'

Something flitted across her friend's expression just then. Something so dark and bleak that it caught her unprepared.

'He was there?' Bas choked. 'You met him?'

Did Bas know? Was that what this was about? But even if he did, why would he care?

'I did,' she admitted tightly, not understanding where the sudden animosity had come from. 'Is there some reason I shouldn't have?'

'He was actually there?' Bas was practically snarling at her now. 'He had the bloody audacity? And you didn't think to call me? You didn't think to even mention it?'

What on earth was she missing? It made no sense.

'I rather thought you had enough going on,' she managed jerkily. 'Don't you?'

'Not more important than Henrik turning up,' her friend roared.

Grace froze. Her mind wasn't so much racing, as it was hurtling around her skull, wholly out of control. He couldn't possibly mean...

'Wait. *Henrik?*' she echoed slowly. 'You mean Rik?'

She knew about Henrik. She was possibly one of the only people with whom Bas had shared stories about his past—just as she had shared hers with him—but Henrik Jansen certainly wasn't an individual Grace had ever cared to meet.

The way he'd betrayed his brother—even as kids—had been horrific.

'Rik?'

'Dr Rik Magnusson,' she managed, though her tongue felt far too unwieldy for her mouth. 'The new surgeon.'

Oh, Lord...but she hadn't just met him. She'd slept with him.

No, it still didn't make sense. It couldn't.

A wave of nausea swelled in Grace's belly, and there was no missing the fury in her friend's glower.

He snorted.

'That's what he's calling himself?'

This couldn't be happening. She couldn't quite process it.

'When you say Henrik, you don't mean...?' She stopped awkwardly, afraid that she sounded dumb. 'But he called himself Rik. And surely he would be a Jansen?'

'My father's name is Magnus.' Bas bit out every word as though it pained him. It certainly hurt her, to think that she'd contributed to her friend's anguish. 'Presumably, he thinks he's clever calling himself Magnusson. And shortening Henrik to Rik.'

Grade didn't want to believe it, however much

it fitted. But then, the expression on her friend's face—that flicker of hesitation—made her wonder if he'd remembered something else.

'Perhaps he's trying to be discreet,' she managed hopefully. 'Maybe he's trying not to cause a scene.'

'If he doesn't want a scene, then he shouldn't have come here. He should have stayed the hell away, just as he has done these past thirty years. Just as he ought to have done when I didn't answer any of his letters.'

Except that her friend's tone lacked the absolute anger of a moment ago. As though he was a little less sure.

Grace swallowed down a cry of exasperation. If only Bas had said something, if only he'd *told* her, then she could have been on her guard for Rik… Henrik.

She'd known Bas for too long, her loyalty to him was absolute. However strong the attraction to Rik, that night of the gala, had she known his true identity she would never have risked her friendship for a one-night stand.

Not even one as glorious as the other night had been.

But, dammit, Bas hadn't told her a thing. The guilt she'd felt before was being chased now by anger. If her friend hadn't been so closed off—if he'd trusted her enough to confide in her—then this would never have happened.

'Rik wrote to you?' she demanded fiercely before she could check herself.

But how she wished she could bite the words back when the infamous black gaze bored into her, skewering her in place.

A different colour from Rik's green-blue eyes, admittedly, but how could she have failed to see the similarities between the two men? Notably, that characteristic, all-commanding expression.

But then, Bas had never made her feel as sensual, as all-woman, as Rik had. Her friend had come into her life at a time when she'd needed precisely that—a friend. Ultimately, he'd made her feel as if he were a protective big brother.

Rik had made her feel something quite, quite sublimely different.

'Rik?' Bas demanded harshly, yanking her attention back into the room. 'You're acquainted with him?'

The silence stretched out so very long between them.

Part of her wanted to confess the truth, perhaps even explain herself. But another part of her—a stronger part—wanted to hold onto the sweet perfection of her weekend with Rik. Even if only for a little bit longer.

But even now, she feared that memory was tarnished for good. Because however glorious it had been with Rik, however much she'd hoped something more might have come of it, the ugly truth was that he'd lied to her.

He wasn't Rik Magnusson—he was Henrik Jansen. Brother to the person she thought of as her closest friend.

The one man who was utterly off-limits to her. Her heart hammered harder against her ribs— enough to bruise. And yet she drew in a deep breath and mentally squared herself. She might not know what was going on here, but she knew she didn't deserve to be attacked.

'I didn't know who he was,' she cried out at last.

But the implication was clear and her friend's face turned to disgust.

'You had sex with him?' he said coldly. 'Of all the people in this hospital, in this county, with whom you could have had sex, you chose my brother?'

'How could I have known?' Grace thrust her hands in her hair.

The worst of it was that she wasn't sure what she was most angry about. That she'd hurt her friend? That Bas hadn't trusted her? Or was it that something inside her died at the thought of not being able to see Rik again?

She thought it was that possibility that shamed her above all others.

'I asked you to go in my place and to look out

for anything unusual. Anyone who was there who shouldn't be.'

For a long moment, they stood watching each other. And then Grace's panic began to die down, and she eyed him critically.

'And from that, I was supposed to know you meant your brother?'

He gritted his teeth at her.

'Anyone unusual, Grace.'

'I couldn't possibly have known that meant the brother you haven't seen in almost thirty years. I couldn't possibly have concluded that the stranger I happened to meet—the perfectly...normal man, who called himself Rik and was a surgeon like so many people at that medical ball—was the someone *unusual*.'

Another disdainful snort was directed her way. But she didn't care.

'You think you *happened* to meet him? That it was a coincidence that he bumped into you—the person I'm closest to?'

It took her a moment to work out what he was saying. And when she did, she felt that nausea from before beginning to rise. She shook her head as vigorously as she could.

As if that could stop his words from being true.

'You're saying he sought me out deliberately?' she whispered, her words jagged.

For a long time, he didn't speak. Grace could

practically see the wheels in his head spinning around.

But she couldn't say anything. Or do anything. She was still feverishly trying to process the last thing Bas had said. Trying to make sense of it.

Had Rik... *Henrik*...really used her? Had he known exactly who she was when he'd approached her at that gala? Had he slept with her because he'd thought she was a way to get to his brother?

Her gut screamed that it wasn't true. That wasn't the man she'd met. She opened her mouth to tell her friend, but then she stopped. And she swallowed her denial.

Because she wasn't exactly renowned for her ability to read people, was she?

Grace opened her mouth again, this time to apologise. But Bas started speaking before she could.

'I have to go. But you need to meet up with Henrik again.'

She cast him a horrified glance.

'What? *No!*'

'Yes.' He nodded grimly. 'Whatever he's doing here, whatever he's up to, I need to know.'

Grace gaped at him, appalled.

'Wait, you want me to spy on Henrik? I can't. No. If you want to know why Henrik's here, Bas, you're going to have to speak to him.'

He glanced at her, but seemed entirely un-moved.

'Please, Grace, I'm asking you as my friend. Whatever Henrik is doing here, it won't be good. But I have to concentrate on Naomi right now. She has to be my priority. My baby has to be my main focus.'

'Bas...' Grace bit her lip. 'What you're asking...'

What made it all the more abhorrent was that there was a sliver of her that welcomed the excuse to see Rik again. Despite everything.

What awful things must that say about her?

'I'm not asking you to sleep with him again, for pity's sake,' Bas snapped, as if reading her thoughts. 'I'm just asking you to occupy him. Distract him. Maybe show him around the hospital. Take him on a tour of the city.'

'Show him around...' she echoed uncertainly.

'You could even ask him to take my place in the hospital fete this year.'

'You really want Rik... Henrik, to get involved in the charitable side of the hospital?'

'Not particularly.' Bas gritted his teeth. 'But you know how long the prep work takes, between repairing the stalls and giving the tired ones a fresh lick of paint. And then there's the manning of them. It takes time. All of which I could be spending with Naomi this year.'

Her head was such a jumble that she couldn't think straight.

If she agreed, would she be agreeing on her friend's terms? Or merely because it meant she didn't have to stop seeing the first man who'd made her feel alive in a long, long time.

The only man.

'I don't know, Bas.' Grace pursed her lips.

'You slept with my brother, Grace. I think you owe me.'

That was below the belt. Especially for the man who had been her only true friend for the better part of a decade. But though she wanted to, she didn't dare argue for fear that she might betray more than she wanted to. Even to herself.

Perhaps she could do it. As much to get answers to her own questions as to get answer to Bas's. Like, had Rik known who she was that night? Had he used her?

The very thought of it made her feel sick. No, there was no choice—she couldn't possibly agree.

It would be the second time she'd been used by someone in such an intimate way. But at least the fact that Rik had used protection meant that she wouldn't pay the ultimate price this time.

She wouldn't end up spending a lifetime wondering, and searching, and hoping for someone else.

One was enough.

Without warning, grief slammed into her. And with it, guilt.

She owed Bas so much. If it hadn't been for

him, she wasn't sure she'd be where she was now. Certainly not here—a sought-after obstetrics doctor at a hospital with ties to one of the country's most prestigious private medical centres.

Before that propitious day when she'd first met Bas, the nineteen-year-old, first-year medical student that she'd been had been just about ready to throw in the towel. If not on life, then certainly on any idea of a fulfilling career.

She hadn't thought she'd deserved it.

But Bas had rescued her. He'd pulled her out of the dark, sinking pit that had been claiming her, inch by inch, for years—even if he'd never known it. Even if she'd never been able to share her terrible secret with him.

She owed him. And if spying on his brother—the one man who had made her feel physically alive, for the first time since she'd been sixteen—was the dues she had to pay, then she would do it.

'Okay,' she heard herself mutter quietly, at length. 'Okay, I'll do it. I'll try to keep him distracted. But there's a time limit, Bas. I'll give you a week.'

'A month,' he countered, though he sounded as grim as she felt.

A shiver ran through her. Though, Grace suspected, not for any of the reasons it really ought to. Because she could tell herself it was her penance, but that didn't stop some perfidious part of her from thinking that she might actually enjoy *having* to spend time with Rik.

'A fortnight,' she managed. 'So you'd better do the right thing by Naomi, Bas. And you'd better agree on your solution quickly.'

Because she was terribly afraid that the longer she spent with Rik, the easier it would be to forget why she had agreed to it in the first place.

She needed answers. Not to fall for the last man on Earth that she should find attractive.

'Agreed.' Bas offered a terse nod and made his way to the door. 'And, Grace, thank you.'

A moment later, he was gone, leaving Grace all alone. And as if it couldn't get much worse, her phone started to vibrate in her pocket.

She didn't know how she sensed it would be Rik, even as she slid her shaking hands into the fabric to retrieve it. Still, she stared at the ringing screen for a moment before shutting it off.

How had she gone from looking forward to spending time with the magnificent Rik, to spying on the hated Henrik, in the space of a few minutes?

It was too much.

Agreement or not, she needed to cancel their dates—the surgical date as well as the dinner date—until she got her head straight again and figured out precisely how she was supposed to spend time with Rik without him realising that something was now very wrong.

CHAPTER SEVEN

LEANING ON THE DOORFRAME, wondering when he'd last done something so out of character, Rik lifted his knuckles to the wooden door and knocked. Loudly.

Moments later it swung open and Grace stood in front of him, barefoot and ponytail swinging.

It should ring alarm bells how possessive that made him feel.

'I do have neighbours, you know...' she began, then tailed off when she saw it was him. 'Oh, I thought you were someone else.'

Something knotted in Rik's gut as he took in the worry lines that were suddenly etched into Grace's lovely face. Something was wrong. She hadn't cancelled their dates because of a patient-related emergency—his instinct had been spot-on.

To be fair, it usually was, but this time he'd really hoped he'd misread the situation.

'Who were you expecting?' he asked, before he could stop himself.

Lightly, non-aggressively, so she couldn't see how desperate he was to know—as uncharacteristic of himself as it felt to even care.

She hesitated, as though she wasn't going to answer. The knot pulled tighter.

Finally, she relented.

'I thought you were my grocery delivery,' she confessed after a moment.

And it shouldn't have made him anything like as relieved.

'Good. Then I can come in?'

It didn't escape him the way her eyes kept sliding from his, as though she found it too hard to look straight at him. As though she was…fighting with herself.

Or perhaps that was just what he wanted to think.

'I'd rather you didn't.' She stood in the doorway as if to block him.

In effect, however, the action brought her—and her body—all too mouth-wateringly close. And by the way her pulse beat erratically at the base of her smooth, elegant neck, he wasn't the only one feeling that familiar rush of heat.

It practically sizzled through the air between them.

Was he to take heart from the knowledge that whatever had caused her to cancel their dates—both medical and personal—it wasn't because she'd decided she was no longer attracted to him?

'Do you want to tell me what's going on?'

At least his voice was even, back to his usual control. Even if inside felt like a jumble of unfamiliar emotions.

Her eyes flickered to his—just for a split second—and then dropped away again.

'I'm career-focussed at the moment,' she bit out, as though it was a speech she'd been rehearsing but couldn't quite commit to. 'I don't have time for…flirtations.'

'Rubbish.'

He didn't intend to move but suddenly his fingers were under her chin, tilting it up so that he could look right into those expressive eyes of hers. And this heat between them was so intense that it glowed blinding white.

The force of it walloped into him, practically knocking him off his feet.

'Fine…' Her breath was a whisper that he might have felt, more than heard. 'Perhaps we should start with the fact that your name is actually Henrik Jansen.'

'Ahh.'

Guilt moved through him.

'*Ahh*, indeed,' Grace echoed, but her voice shook a little beneath the surface. 'Bas is my friend and you're his brother. A fact about which you clearly lied to me.'

'Not lied,' he qualified, hating his own words in that moment. 'Omitted.'

'That's your apology?'

Her expression grew disdainful, and the sense of guilt that had been rumbling quietly through him now grew.

'You're right.' He held his hands up, palms outstretched, in front of her. 'And I do want to apologise.'

As if that could magic it all away.

There was a beat of silence, as though she thought the same thing.

'Then why did you do it?' she asked, when he didn't offer anything further. 'Did you target me because you already knew he and I were friends? Was I your way to get closer to him?'

'No,' he ground out, abhorring the suspicion in her expression.

As well as the fact that he was the one who had put it there.

It made him wonder how many people had used Grace in the past, in order to get closer to the infamous Bas. Women—undoubtedly, given his brother's womanising reputation, but men? Possibly—especially if they were surgeons wanting to learn from someone with his brother's reputation and skill.

And Grace was glowering at him.

'Then was sleeping with me your way of getting under your brother's skin?'

'That's absurd,' he bit out, riled despite his attempts to stay calm.

Another chink in his usually irreproachable control. What was it about this woman?

'Is it?' she cried. 'Bas believes—'

'*Bas* believes?' he echoed incredulously, though a lot quieter than Grace. '*My brother* is the one who put such a damned insulting idea in your head?'

'He's looking out for me.'

'He is looking out for himself,' Rik ground out, even as he hated himself for letting those old fears sneak out.

He tried valiantly to stuff them back. He hadn't come all this way to resurrect an old argument with his long-lost brother. On the contrary, this trip—all this effort—was supposed to be about healing. Funny how one woman could put all that at risk. He ought to walk away right now.

But he couldn't.

Instead, he stood motionless, waiting for her to speak. To answer his question.

But Grace didn't say a word. Instead, the lift of her shoulders was almost delicate. And a part of him longed to answer her—to explain himself—but then there was something else moving through him, too. Something strange.

Something that—had he not known better— he might have mistaken for a sliver of jealousy.

But of course that couldn't be the case. She was a one-night—weekend—stand. There was no reason for jealousy to figure into it. He opened his mouth to say something practical. Logical.

'What's really going on here?' his voice cracked out instead, the low tone doing nothing to soften that almost lethal edge. 'Are you worried I will tell him about your little indiscretion?'

'My…indiscretion?'

That unwelcome, misplaced sensation slithered around the pit of Rik's belly. He'd never known anything like it before. He certainly didn't like it.

And still, he was powerless to stop it.

'Come now, I think we can dispense with the games. It's clear you're preoccupied with what will happen when Bas hears about your night with me.'

'No,' she denied quickly. 'That isn't true.'

'Then you would take no issue with him knowing that happened between us?'

'None…' She bit her lip uncertainly.

'As I thought,' Rik cut in with an expression of disgust.

Though less at her, and more at himself.

'Wait…no,' she cried out quietly as he swung abruptly away from her. 'It isn't like…that.'

'More lies, *älskling*?'

Grace blinked, momentarily stunned, and the slithering and churning sensations intensified.

'Let me guess, my brother uses that same phrase—*älskling*—and you thought it was unique to you?'

What was the matter with him? Why couldn't he stop talking? It was so out-of-character for him, but then his usual iron will had deserted him from that first night he'd met Grace.

'I've heard Bas use it,' she admitted. 'Though rarely. And certainly not to me.'

'Is that right?' he added.

And finally, finally, Grace jerked her head up to meet his eye.

'I told you once before that he and I have only ever been friends.'

'Given his reputation, I find that hard to believe.'

Although he wanted to believe her. Perhaps more than he'd ever wanted to believe anything—though that made no sense.

'Then, regrettably, that's something for you to reconcile,' Grace said quietly. 'Not me.'

The weight of her soulful gaze was almost too much for him to stand. He still wanted her. Even now. Even though he couldn't explain this dark, covetous thing that moved inside him.

'We are both adults here.' He had no idea how he kept his tone so mild. 'We had sex—incredible sex, I might add, in which you screamed out my name many times—but now that you know who I am, it seems you're desperate for my brother not to find out what happened. If you and he are not together, explain that to me, if you will.'

He waited as she chewed on the inside of her cheek, and shifted her weight first from one side, and then the next. And then, when she still didn't answer, he decided he needed to intervene…just as a movement dragged his attention away and he snapped his head around. A blur of grey-green was hurtling down the corridor to the lift doors at the end, just as they pinged and began to close.

'Cooper!'

As Grace cried out, Rik didn't even pause to think. He spun around and chased down the corridor after the flying missile, throwing himself into the lift just as the doors closed. He scooped the grey-green blob into his arms and realised it was a young cat. And for all its athletic display a few moments earlier, it was quite a friendly one at that—purring contentedly the moment he tickled its chin.

By the time he got back to Grace's floor, it—Cooper, if he remembered correctly—was virtually his best friend.

He strode up the corridor, half expecting Grace to yell at him for frightening her pet. Half looking forward to it, if he was going to be honest, because at least it meant she would no longer be trying to ignore him.

Instead, she laughed ruefully as he strode up the corridor and, just like that, the ice was broken again between them.

'Yours, I presume?' He held out the wriggling feline.

'Thank you.' She reached out to take it. 'Though you didn't have to break your neck to catch him. He would have been okay.'

Rik might have frowned, but at least the unexpected interlude had broken the ice between him and Grace again. For that, he was grateful.

'From the way you called his name when he escaped, I thought you were afraid he would get himself lost.'

'He startled me, that's all.' She shook her head. 'He goes out a fair bit. Sometimes to my neighbour across the hall because she has a cat, too. And lots of cat treats. And sometimes out of the window. It's one of the perks of having a ground-floor apartment that backs onto hectares of woodland. Thank you, though. It was very sweet of you to chase after him.'

'I ought to object to being called *sweet*...' He arched his eyebrows. 'But if it's enough for you to now invite me in...?'

Grace bit her lip, then stepped back in tacit agreement as she placed the cat—who now seemed content to stay inside the apartment—onto the floor. Rik stepped through as she closed the door behind them.

'You haven't had him long, I take it? Cooper, I mean.'

'He's eleven years old.'

'Really?' Surprised, Rik eyed the cat a little closer. 'I thought he was much younger.'

'He's small,' Grace acknowledged. 'But he's still very active.'

Her soft smile was almost proud. Clearly Cooper was a good way to her heart.

'How did you come to have him?'

'I've had him since a kitten.' She seemed to pause before plunging on. 'Bas has his brother.'

Rik stopped, not sure he'd heard properly. Not certain of the implications. But he didn't need to ask more, since Grace was already speaking again.

'It was a summer night, just as it was starting to go dark, when we were on our way back from the hospital one night. As we passed the canal, Bas saw a plastic bag under the bridge and... I don't know what he saw, or whether it was instinct, but the next thing I knew, he was scrambling over thorny undergrowth. When he opened the rubbish bag, there were three kittens inside. One had clearly died, but the other two were alive. Though barely.'

'My brother rescued abandoned kittens?'

It was so unlike the man he'd been hearing about these past few years, yet so like the brother he remembered. Especially that impetuous boy who had always thrown himself into whatever he'd perceived as the right thing to do, without ever thinking twice.

Sometimes, without even thinking it through.

'We took the kittens to the local vets,' Grace continued, 'who said that the remaining two kittens were really too small, and too weak, to survive. That they would need round-the-clock care and that, sadly, they simply didn't have the staff or resources to do it right then.'

'So my brother took them on, did he not?'

Rik knew the answer without her even needing to tell him. He could well imagine the brother he had known staying up, night and day, to care for them. To tend to them.

'He did.' Grace nodded. 'They needed feeding every two to three hours initially, and Bas took that on. He risked his place on the course to care for them—not that it mattered academically since he was way ahead of the rest of us anyway, partly due to having Magnus as a father, and partly due to Bas's own innate ability. I tried to help whenever I could, but I couldn't afford to risk my education the way Bas did.'

'So Magnus was a good father to Bas?'

It was odd, the way that knowledge made him feel relieved, and yet twisted and scraped at him, all at once.

Relieved, because Bas had got the parent he deserved, after what their mother had put him—an innocent kid—through, but bitter because, at the end of the day, he himself had never been able to escape her. Or her cruelty.

But Grace's expression changed and became closed off.

'You would need to speak to Bas about his relationship with Magnus.'

'It must have been relatively good,' Rik pressed. 'You don't take time out of a medical degree to care for a couple of kittens, without risking your education.'

Grace bristled, and, even though he could see she didn't want to rise to his comment, he needed to know more. To understand.

'I imagine having Magnus guiding him has been a bonus,' Rik noted evenly.

Grace glowered at him.

'The Jansen father-son team is certainly world-renowned,' he continued. 'I think everyone has heard the stories about how the great Magnus Jansen would bring his ten-year-old son to the OR to watch operations.'

'You shouldn't believe everything you read,' she managed, her voice stilted.

And it only made him all the keener to learn more. To know that Bas had landed on his feet with the father who hadn't had anything to do with either of them during the first seven years of their lives. Which was, at the end of the day, why he'd left Stockholm to come here—if only for a few months.

And to understand exactly what the nature of this woman's relationship with his brother was—which *wasn't* why he'd come here.

'So you're saying the stories aren't true?' he pressed her, mercilessly. 'That Magnus didn't help Bas?'

'Yes, they're true,' she gritted out, at last. 'And of course that exposure has helped to make Bas the surgeon he is today. But that has always been about your father's ego.'

'I believe Bas is the one with an ego.'

'No. Maybe. But Bas is all about the patient. And taking him to surgeries was all fine when Bas was a kid, idolising his hero surgeon father.' She swallowed, but forced herself to continue. 'But what I'm saying is that Magnus didn't do him any favours once Bas turned eighteen and went to uni to study medicine. And your father certainly didn't do Bas any favours when it came to starting plastics as a speciality.'

'Bas is here, isn't he? Running the private Jansen wing at this hospital. His name above the door. His reputation intact as one of the country's fastest rising surgeons in his field?'

'You really ought to talk with your brother about this,' she told him desperately.

'I'm talking to you,' Rik pointed out. 'Since you seem to have a vested interest.

She bared her teeth at him. Actually bared them. And it might have had an impact, had he not immediately imagined them pressed against his naked flesh.

As if he were a man possessed.

'No vested interest,' she bit out, bending down to stroke the cat.

It took him a moment to realise this was her attempt at regrouping.

'You seem pretty clued up on my brother,' he

countered. But this time, some of the heat had gone out of his tone.

Enough to let Grace relax a little.

'All I can tell you is that Bas had to be twice as good as any other surgeon for his father to even allow him into the Jansen wing. Your father only really allowed him any say when he realised that Bas being there brought in more money than ever. And money is what motivates your father.'

'And it doesn't motivate Bas?' Rik scoffed.

'Not particularly.' She stood firm. 'Bas is all about the patients, every time.'

'And the women, of course. Don't forget his playboy reputation.'

He saw the temper swirl beneath her skin moments before it burst out.

'Listen, *Henrik*, you might think you know Bas from all the rumours, and stories, but you don't. You haven't been in his life for almost thirty years, but I can tell you that Bas never really had a childhood. He didn't go to parties, or have friends over, he grew up with nannies, or in observation galleries to operating rooms as Magnus performed his surgeries. The only things that interested Magnus were his career, and women.'

'Like father, like son, then.'

'Not really. But if it makes you feel better to think that, then go ahead. Bas is twice the man you are, by all accounts.'

'Why? Because he risked it all in order to raise

two kittens, like some kind of rebellion?' Rik threw back scornfully.

He couldn't have said why. Though he suspected it was because he didn't want to accept the fact that he'd spent the past thirty years believing that it didn't matter that he'd lost his brother—his best friend, and the best anchor he'd had in his life—because Bas had a better life with his father.

'No,' Grace denied, dragging him back to the present. 'I think it was his attempt to capture the youth he'd never had.'

'Why?'

But Grace was already clamming up, clearly regretting having said anything at all.

'All I can tell you is that Bas was already years ahead of anyone else on the course and had perfect scores in almost everything he did, so any attempts to get him kicked out of uni ultimately failed. The kittens—who were never supposed to have survived—began to thrive. We named them Sonny, and Cooper, and Bas has one whilst I have the other.'

Something clicked suddenly in Rik's head. Something else, pushing its way through the fog that had suddenly dropped in his brain.

'So when you say you're friends with Bas, you don't mean as colleagues.'

'No, I mean as friends.' She wiped her hand over her forehead. 'Good friends. The kind you trust with your life.'

He hesitated. His thoughts might as well have been trying to race through treacle.

'I didn't appreciate that.'

'I know. But I meant it, the other night, when I told you that if it hadn't been for Bas, I wouldn't be a doctor today. You didn't believe me, but it isn't exaggeration, it's a fact.'

'Then I apologise for that, too,' he told her sincerely. 'Perhaps we could start over. I'm Henrik Magnusson.'

He held his hand out, waiting for her to take it.

'You're lying, even now,' she cried instead, heading for the door and yanking it back open again. 'You're not Magnusson at all, are you? You're Jansen. Henrik *Jansen*.'

And what did it say that he wanted, so badly, to defend himself on that score, at least?

'As far as my name goes, I didn't lie to you,' he heard himself saying. 'The reason I didn't introduce myself as Henrik Jansen was because, up until a few months ago, I didn't even know that was my father's real name. I was brought up as Henrik Magnusson.'

'But, what about Bas?'

'He was called Bas Magnusson, whether he remembers it now, or not,' Rik told her firmly. 'At first, I didn't mention Bas being my brother because I wanted to speak with him before I told anyone else who I was. It was the only reason I was at the gala that night.'

'Even when I told you that he and I were friends?'

'I'd heard enough about his playboy reputation already. How could I have known that you were genuinely so close?'

'Yet you pursued me. Why? Because you thought I was your way to your brother? How selfish do you have to be to do that, Rik?'

'It wasn't like that.'

He kept his hand out. But although Grace stared at it for an inordinately long time, she didn't take it.

Instead, at last, she shook her head.

'I can't. I won't. Bas and I will always be there for each other, because I owe him that much. And because he is my friend.'

'Just as he's my brother.'

'No. No, he isn't,' she gritted out, feeding that dark, icy thing that had squatted inside him for as long as he could remember. 'Because you...don't exist to him. Not after what you did.'

The words slammed into Rik.

Everything he'd been beginning to fear was being all wrapped up in one.

Did his brother genuinely believe that he had been the victim, even though he'd been the one to escape? How could Bas hate him so much that he pretended not to even have a brother?

It made no sense, but, more than that, it made Rik feel a hurt and a vulnerability that he'd refused to feel for decades. A weakness that he'd learned to stuff down the day that his brother had been taken from him.

He'd thought he'd ripped down his heart a long time ago. Thought he'd buried it in the deepest, darkest black hole where it could never be found. Because that way no one could ever hurt him again.

But hearing what his brother—his beloved, morally upright brother, who he'd idolised his entire life—had said about him, Rik felt an overwhelming urge to lean on the wall behind him, and just let his legs go until he slid down it to the floor.

The way he'd done as a kid—just once—before his brother had hauled him to his feet and made him swear that he'd never, *never* let their mother, or anyone, make him feel as if he was nothing, ever again.

Instead, Rik stood his ground. Because weakness wasn't even in his vocabulary any more.

'You don't exist to Bas,' Grace was saying, and he didn't know if it was her gritted teeth, or the tumult in his own head, that was muffling her words. 'So, you don't exist to me. Now please, leave.'

And even though a thousand things cluttered up his brain, and his chest, they were woven so tightly that he couldn't unpick them. He didn't even know where to begin.

So Rik did the only thing he could do—he left.

CHAPTER EIGHT

'LET'S PREP THE patient for CT, and get a good set of images for me,' Rik instructed, as he left the resus bay to contact another senior plastic surgeon who he knew was on call. 'I'm going to need them to work out whether there are any bones left in there, and what I can work with. And book an OR, please.'

'Do you really think you can save anything of the patient's hand?' A resident caught him as he left the area, making sure they were both out of earshot of the patient or his screaming family. 'There's nothing there. I've seen patients with injuries not even as severe as this that surgeons have deemed unsalvageable.'

'And for them, that may be true,' Rik answered without pomp. 'It certainly looks bad, but I believe I can give him something of a hand.'

Though it would be no mean feat. One look at the man's extremity had shown that it had been almost severed in two places and was only still attached thanks to the faintest sliver of skin and bone. If he were to stand any chance of saving his patient's hand, he was going to have to start as quickly as possible, before everything turned necrotic.

Establishing good blood and nerve supply to

the fingers would be vital. And he'd sewn hands and feet, even ears and nose, to groins before now, in an attempt to save dying body parts.

He tried his colleague a few times, but there was no answer. He would have to put in a call to the Jansen wing and see if anyone from Plastics was on call up there.

Hopefully not his father or brother.

Shoving the phone into his pocket, Rik strode quickly back to the resus bay, in time to hear his brother speaking to the ward sister, just his side of the curtain.

'Book an OR.'

It seemed that someone had already contacted the Jansen wing, and that fate had decided to play a prank on him. But there was no time to take it personally. His patient was depending on him to do everything in his power to save the remnants of his hand.

With a steadying breath, Rik stepped forward, his voice calm. Controlled.

'It's booked.'

His brother froze, then turned slowly.

And Rik felt as though everything had stopped.

He'd spent years—decades—imagining this moment. But now that it was here, it felt surreal.

The eyes were the same colour that he remembered, but the expression in them was nothing like the love and care his brother used to have for him.

'Henrik,' his brother bit out icily. 'What the hell are you doing here?'

Rik opened his mouth to speak, but realised that all the questions charging around his head were in Swedish. He couldn't seem to remember a word of English.

'It is the Jansen exchange programme,' he began. 'I have been writing to you three times.'

His brother worked his jaw a few times. The look of hostility in his regard every bit as harsh as before.

'I am aware. It landed me with the task of having to throw them in the trash where they belong,' he clipped out, making Rik wince. Though not through any weakness, but more because it was heartbreaking to hear the bitterness in his brother's voice. 'My mistake—what I really meant to say was, get away from my case.'

'The way I am to keep away from Grace?' Rik asked softly, though his brother would have to be an idiot to miss the steely core of his tone.

Bas eyeballed him.

'Grace is a grown woman. She makes her own decisions. And I never told her to stay away from you.'

'No,' Rik agreed easily enough. 'You merely told her that I have targeted her because I knew you two were friends.'

'I can't imagine Grace told you that.' Bas narrowed his eyes, though he didn't deny it.

Rik hadn't expected that he would. His brother had never been a liar.

'Of course not,' Rik replied. 'She is loyal to you. But she asked me, and I knew it had come from you.'

'Perhaps so. But it wasn't a lie, was it?'

There were so many things that Rik wanted to say to that. But instead, he had to content himself with sticking to the basic facts. And not only because they didn't have much time to talk whilst their patient was on his way to CT.

'I went to that medical ball to talk to you, Basilius. I did not know who Grace was when I first spoke to her that night.'

Bas eyed him shrewdly, but Rik had no intention of backing down.

'But you knew who she was when you slept with her. Didn't you?'

Rik didn't answer—he didn't believe his brother's question dignified one. But he certainly didn't expect Bas to take that as confirmation.

'As I thought,' Bas spat out, disgusted, and a sudden anger shot through Rik.

'What is Grace to you, Basilius? Do you love her?'

Bas stopped, taken aback.

'Grace is a friend,' he rasped. 'Nothing more. Has she not told you that?'

Rik eyed him in frank assessment.

'That's exactly what she told me. But I'm not

a fool, brother. I know you sent her to watch me. What is your saying? *Keep your enemies close?*'

'Something like that,' Bas murmured.

'So, I shall ask you again, do you care for her, Basilius? Because I think I might, and I am willing to fight for her.'

He wasn't sure which of them was more shocked at the unexpected declaration, and when his brother didn't respond, for a moment, Rik thought Bas had actually listened to what he was saying.

But then a sneer curled his brother's upper lip, like a scalpel to Rik's chest.

'You're not capable of fighting for her. Or anyone.' Bas snorted, making no attempt to conceal his disdain. 'You don't know what love is, Henrik. Neither of us do. The only thing we know is that sick, twisted version of love that we learned from *them.*'

And Rik didn't care what his brother said about their mother, or the man she'd passed off as their father for years. Instead, what scraped at Rik the most was that his brother—the one person in the world who had always had his back as a kid—no longer believed in him. Not at all.

A kind of sadness settled down on Rik, like a heavy, wet, woollen cloak worn in a lightning storm. It offered no solace. Only a depressing weight.

'Is that what you really believe?' he demanded quietly.

'It's what I know.' Bas glowered. 'She might have favoured you, but it didn't make her idea of love any less dangerous. There were always strings attached to her affection.'

'And what about Mrs P? And Bertie?' Rik shook his head, unable to accept that his brother was dismissing them so easily. So heartlessly. 'Were there always strings attached to their love? Or have you forgotten them, Basilius?'

Surely his brother couldn't have buried all the memories of the sweet, kindly Mrs P. The cook who had lived down the road from them, up until they were about seven. Could Bas really have forgotten how Mrs P, and her husband, Bertie, who had worked in the mechanics garage nearby, had treated the two young boys like the children they'd never had?

With kindness. And care. And *love*.

They'd been the stable family that he and Bas had never had. Until their own mother had grown jealous and reacted with her predictable volatility.

'They deserted us,' Bas bit out, and it took Rik a moment to realise that his brother was talking about Mrs P. About Bertie.

And from the bleak expression in his eyes, Bas genuinely thought he knew what he was saying was the truth.

'They didn't leave,' Rik told him softly. 'We left. We went from that suburban house to that flat in the city. Don't you remember?'

His brother shook his head tersely. But there was something in the turn of his face that made Rik think his memory might be beginning to kick back into action.

'Mother was always so jealous of them,' he prompted his brother. 'The way we always used to go to them first for things. Don't you recall running into their kitchen on the way home from school and they'd be waiting to hear about our day, with milk and home-baked fairy cakes? Sometimes, we got to decorate them.'

Bas blinked and, to Rik's shock, he thought he saw tears in his brother's eyes. But then Bas blinked again and they were gone. An unyielding expression taking over his features as he folded his arms over his chest and forced his head up.

It almost made Rik despair. *Almost.*

'Is that why you called me for a consultation on this patient?'

Bas's voice was cold again. Deliberate. But it didn't quite disguise the emotions that Rik suspected lurked beneath the surface.

'I did not call for a consultation,' he denied. 'I was paged.'

'I called for another surgeon.' Rik shrugged. 'I could not have known that would be you. It is an urgent case.' Which was certainly the truth.

It was clear that Bas didn't believe him, but they both knew they couldn't afford to dwell any longer. There wasn't time. There was a patient who needed urgent care and, like it or not, he now had no choice but to work with his brother to save the patient's hand.

'Fine,' Bas growled at length. 'Run me through it.'

It wasn't exactly the breakthrough that Rik had hoped for, but at least it was a start. Swiping his screen to his case notes, Rik passed the tablet over.

'Preliminary tests have been run, and a CT. The sooner I operate the better, but it's likely to run late into the night. Two surgeons working together will make it a faster surgery for the patient. Less time under anaesthetic means less stress on the patient.'

It was the most rational, efficient solution. An operation as this would be likely to be could run to ten, twelve, even fifteen hours. Two surgeons would mean that one surgeon could be harvesting grafts from lower limbs whilst the other worked on the hand. Plus, the less time the patient was under anaesthesia, the better for them.

But he could still see his brother trying to weigh up the pros and cons. Trying to avoid doing the surgery with him, and no doubt trying to find a way that might allow him to take control of it for himself.

There was one thing working at Thorncroft, and the Jansen wing, had revealed about both

Magnus and Bas, and that was their inability to share cases.

'I've seen cases like this before, but this is probably one of the worst cases I've seen,' Bas stated in a clipped tone, which was nonetheless too quiet to be heard by the patient, or his family. 'I suggest you pass this case to me to take lead. I can bring in a surgeon on my team to assist.'

Rik watched him, but opted not to speak. Not until he knew exactly what plan his brother was hatching. As sad as that was.

So much for them having worked together. It wasn't supposed to have been this way.

'If you don't feel able to assist me…' Rik lowered his voice without losing any of his own self-control '…then by all means send another member of your team. However, I have completed several of these procedures in the past. The last case I worked on involved cutting a flap of skin from the groin to embed my patient's hand, to allow the skin to grow and provide new covering.'

Bas stiffened and, with a jolt, Rik realised that his brother agreed with him. He just didn't want to admit it out loud.

'You've harvested veins and nerve grafts from the foot and forearm, to reconstruct the hand?'

'And joined tendons and arteries, yes,' Rik confirmed neutrally. 'As I know you have. So it is up to you to choose whether to work with me on this patient, or not. But right now, I really need to get him into surgery. The sooner I can re-establish blood supply, the better his recovery is likely to be. Are you joining me, or sending someone else?'

It galled Bas that he was right—that much was obvious. Evidently, Bas wasn't accustomed to playing second surgeon to another plastics guy. But then, neither was he. And this was his patient, not Bas's. Personal feelings aside, there was no way the surgeon in him could give that up.

'I've worked on these microsurgical repairs many times before,' Bas stated. 'It's quite draining. You'll need to be good.'

'As will you.'

They met each other's gazes and Rik wondered how pathetic it was that neither of them wanted to be the first one to blink. He wasn't much surprised when his brother took another high-handed tone.

'You have to be realistic about his prognosis. This will never be a normal hand, but, with time and effort, physio can help him regain strength.'

'I made his family clear that even holding a pen will be good progress,' Rik agreed, refusing to rise to the bait. 'He'll need multiple surgeries over the next few months, even years.'

'In time perhaps we can go for a power grip.'

It took Rik a supreme effort not to grin. Despite everything, Bas was echoing exactly the same thought that he himself had entertained.

And if they were in agreement, then it would make working together on the case that much easier.

'In time,' Rik agreed carefully. 'Either way, I must take him in and begin now. I need a decision, Basilius. Can you work with me? Or no?'

Bas paused for one fraction of a moment longer before dipping his head in tacit acquiescence. Then, with a signal from himself to the rest of the team, the bay once again became a flurry of activity as they prepped to bring the patient up to Theatre.

They had hours of surgery ahead of them, and, for the first time in a while, Rik found himself actively looking forward to it.

Slowly, methodically, they began, until at last, fourteen hours later, they found themselves peeling off their gowns and gloves, after a successful operation.

'Good surgery,' his brother muttered grudgingly to him, rolling up his gown and gloves and hurling them into the medical waste bin.

Before Rik—still finishing up his debriefing—could reply, he'd marched through the doors of the surgical suite to scrub out.

By the time Rik joined him in the scrubbing out, Bas was already nearly done.

'Very good,' Rik agreed, nonetheless. 'Would you care to join me in telling the family?'

Bas hesitated, and Rik couldn't be sure what

he'd been about to say before his mobile interrupted him. And then he was taking the call and hurrying out of the room without even looking twice.

But it didn't matter. Not really. Because Rik's mind was back to Grace.

Shoving thoughts of Rik from her mind during the daytime was one thing, Grace decided as she hurried through the doors into the resus department and ducked past yet another pair of colleagues who were gossiping about the 'hot new Swedish exchange surgeon'. But trying not think about him at night time was another thing entirely.

Especially after their confrontation at her apartment the other night meant that she'd abjectly failed in her promise to stay close to him and find out what he was really doing at Thorncroft.

No matter how vigilant she had been during the day, he always invaded her dreams at night, inviting her to relive every perfect moment of their forty-eight hours together. And every morning she woke up disconcerted and hot, and feeling as though she'd done anything but enjoy a restful night in her own bed—*alone.*

She was grateful for her work and the welcome distraction it provided for her errant thoughts—if only temporarily. And she felt guilty that she was even grateful for emergencies like this, which engaged her brain more fully.

Searching for the doctor running the shout—the one who had paged her five minutes earlier—Grace made her way quickly across the room.

'You paged Obstetrics?'

The resus doctor turned to her—Alison, a woman Grace knew quite well.

'Hey, Grace. Janine is a twenty-four-year-old in her third trimester, primigravida, brought in with absent foetal sounds, meconium-stained liquor, and non-progressive labour.'

'Okay, but she should have been brought straight to the women and children's wing.'

'Agreed, but she was brought in by ambulance, having already been brought in last night following a low-impact RTA. Patient was in a stationary vehicle in a car park when another vehicle reversed slowly into them. No apparent injuries sustained, however the patient became distressed that it was her father's car. Foetal scans show the baby was in no distress, and she was discharged without need for further treatment.'

'Right.' Grace nodded. 'If there's nothing else, I'll take her through to the labour ward now.'

Most likely the woman would need a caesarean section.

'One thing.' Alison beckoned her over, lowering her voice. 'The patient has significant childhood post-burn contracture of abdomen, which I suspect would complicate any C-section.'

'Ah.' Grace absorbed the new information. 'Is she comfortable with me taking a look here?'

'So-so.'

'Understood.'

Stepping forward, Grace smiled at her patient.

'Hello, Janine, I'm Grace. I'm an obstetrician. You're in good hands with my colleagues here, but, if they step out, do you mind if I just take a look at your abdomen?'

The patient glanced at the other medical staff and offered a terse nod, and Grace waited until it was only her and Alison before lifting the gown to inspect the area. For additional discretion, she positioned herself between the curtain and her patient, which seemed to help to gain the young woman's trust.

Alison was right, the childhood burns had clearly been quite severe.

'The contracture of the abdomen is visibly tight,' Grace murmured as casually as she could. 'Can I have a little feel for baby?'

Again, her patient nodded, and Grace began a quick examination.

'Does any of this hurt?'

'No.' The young woman shook her head. 'Is my son going to be okay?'

'You know the sex?' Grace checked, her smile in place.

It was the ideal way to keep the mother distracted and as relaxed as possible whilst she carried out an ultrasound and checked for the heartbeat.

'Yeah, I wanted to know as soon as possible.' The young woman half laughed, half sobbed. 'I picked out names and everything. Please look after my baby.'

'You and baby are in the best place for us to help you,' Grace replied, as upbeat as possible, without making promises she might not be able to keep.

Her examination completed, she carefully lowered the gown and stepped back to Alison, her bright smile in place until they'd let the rest of the team back in and they'd rounded the curtain.

'There is a foetal heartbeat, but he's clearly in distress. I need to deliver the baby now. I'm guessing you contacted Plastics?'

'I did,' Alison confirmed. 'In fact, he's just coming over now.'

But Grace didn't need to turn around to know it was Rik.

Of course it was, because who else would it be?

Every fibre of her body screamed it to her, from the fine hairs on the back of her neck to the way her stomach dipped and soared.

But no matter how they'd left things, and no matter what they'd last said to each other, Grace knew that here, in this scenario, Rik would be nothing but professional.

They both would be.

'Dr Henley. Grace,' he greeted her on cue, before turning to introduce himself to Alison. 'Rik Magnusson.'

'Yes, I've seen you around this week, it's nice to finally meet you. I'm Alison.'

There was nothing remotely unprofessional about her colleague's reaction, but Grace knew her well enough to notice that her smile was a little more...dazzling than usual.

A little flirty.

Grace's chest tightened, though it had no right to do so. Not since the last thing she'd said to Rik had been that he didn't exist to her.

Words that she'd wished a hundred times that she could take back.

But that wasn't possible—because it wasn't just about her. It was about her loyalty to her friend—to Rik's brother. Something that should be perfectly easy to remember.

So why wasn't it?

So instead, she forced herself to be patient whilst Alison caught Rik up with the case, and he then performed his own examination. Several minutes later, they were all back outside the cubicle.

'You saw that the post-burn scarring extends over the abdomen and down to the mons region, with some deformity of the lower area?' Grace asked him quietly, grateful for his unerring professionalism as he turned to look at her.

'I did.'

'Given the foetal heart sounds and the fact that he's in distress, I'd like to perform an emergency caesarean—ideally right now—but I realise any incision might not be easy to close.'

'I agree.' Rik drew in a thoughtful breath. 'Contracture is severe and so reconstruction may be necessary, but if you need to do a C-section now, I can make that happen.'

'You're confident?' Grace asked.

'Yes.' He didn't hesitate. 'I'll run you through the ideal incisions, most likely an inverted T-shape which can extend horizontally as far as the contracture vertically to the mons area. Depending on what we encounter, the rest of the C-section might be able to be completed in the usual way.'

'And if it can?'

'Then the uterus will be repaired and the anterior abdominal wall closed as usual, and then I can re-contour and reshape depending on the extent of the displacement.'

'It's that easy?' Grace was impressed, despite herself.

Though she pretended that she didn't feel a thrill of anticipation at the idea of having to work alongside him.

As if even that little contact could help to

quench this interminable thirst she'd felt, ever since the night he'd left her apartment.

As if a part of her wished she'd complied with Bas's request for her to keep Rik close. But Rik wasn't her enemy—he was Bas's. And she couldn't help but wonder if he was even that.

'It is possible I need to harvest some skin grafts from her thighs.' Rik's voice tugged her back to reality. 'I could also resurface some other areas of her abdomen to reduce the scarring for her.'

'Okay.' She nodded. 'Let's get our patient to Theatre and see if we can't deliver this baby successfully.'

And she wished that traitorous part of her weren't actually looking forward to going into the surgery side by side with this particular man.

CHAPTER NINE

'NICE JOB,' RIK complimented her as he and Grace removed their gloves and gowns and deposited them into the bin, before moving to scrub out.

The baby had been delivered a while ago—remarkably strong and healthy, all things given, and Grace had handed the newborn boy to one of her colleagues to take to the PICU and stayed to assist him with the closure.

Logically, he knew it was because any surgeon would be a fool to pass up such a learning opportunity—the observation room above them was full of residents all eager to fill the vacancy if Grace had vacated it—but there was still a part of him that wanted to believe she'd also stayed because it was him.

Since when had he ever let his ego rule him like this? And yet something sloshed inside him.

'That was…stunning,' Grace qualified.

He wondered what she'd been about to say before she'd caught herself. Surely her words shouldn't heat him in this way? Like the sun permeating his skin and warming up his bones?

'About the other night—'

'I think we should forget it happened,' Rik interrupted quickly. 'Move on, as you say in England.'

'Move on?' She hesitated.

'Or perhaps, start over.'

Grace cast him an indecipherable look.

'I think I'd like that,' she agreed, after a moment.

They both fell silent, and for a moment Rik wondered what to say.

'I can see now why you were selected for the Jansen programme,' Grace burst out awkwardly. 'You're honestly...a great surgeon.'

He grimaced, reading between the lines.

'After everything you told me about Magnus refusing to help Bas become a surgeon, did you believe that he'd given me a place on the programme merely because I'm his other long-lost son?'

She wrinkled her nose, and he wondered if she had any idea how much that quirk made him ache to reach out and smooth the puckered skin.

'I guess not,' she conceded. 'But I couldn't help but wonder.'

With anyone else, he probably wouldn't have cared. But with her, he felt the oddest need to defend himself.

'He did not,' stated Rik simply. 'In truth, I don't even know if he's aware that I'm here. Presumably, he doesn't even read the applicants' files. He must have a team who do all of that for him, as well as make the decision.'

And, if he did know, the man had certainly made no attempt to make contact.

'He knows,' Grace told him. 'No one gets onto any of the three nationwide Jansen Suites without his knowledge. It's his magnum opus, he watches everything that happens.'

'So, then, he has chosen not to bother with me,' Rik noted as Grace bit her lip wryly.

'I'm sorry, I shouldn't—'

'Don't be sorry,' he cut in easily. Truthfully. 'It makes no difference to me. It was Bas I came here to speak with. Not a man I never met.'

'Still...'

'Bas and I were close, and he was the brother that I lost. Magnus was the father I never had to begin with. When my brother was first sent to him, I think I might have harboured some childish hope that he might seek me out. But he didn't. I came to terms, a long time ago, with the fact that he never wanted to know me.'

'His loss,' Grace whispered. Though Rik didn't think she'd intended to.

And suddenly, despite everything he'd said, he felt her empathy slide inside him like a comforting blanket for his bruised soul.

He shut it down quickly. Hating the fact she'd found another chink of weakness in him.

'If it's all the same to you, I'd prefer to reserve this conversation for my brother.'

If Bas ever stopped avoiding him.

'Rik...the things you said, about not even knowing what your real name is...?'

'It is not a conversation we will continue, *älskling*,' he told her firmly. 'That is a conversation between my brother and me.'

'I understand, but Bas believes—'

'You will not be caught in the middle of us,' he cut her off.

If he couldn't do anything else for her, he could do that much. Though he didn't care to examine why it was so important to him.

Neither of them spoke for several minutes. And then, at last, Grace straightened up from the sink.

'There's a fete...a festival. The hospital runs it every year and Bas and I usually help out. This year, he can't.'

'Can't? Or won't?'

'Can't,' she emphasised.

'Why not?'

'It's a long story, and not mine to tell.' She bit her lip, and he couldn't explain why he actually believed her. 'Suffice to say that there's an empty slot if you want to help.'

Despite their improved conversation, the offer wasn't what he'd expected.

He folded his arms over his chest, liking the way her eyes were dragged to the movement, and her nostrils flared slightly. Maybe he liked it too much.

It told him the things that she wasn't saying.

'Is this your idea of an apology?'

'Something like that,' she muttered, as if she was making the admission with difficulty. And he liked that, too. 'Forget it, I shouldn't have asked.'

And that *need* still sloshed around inside him. It was rather too telling that his brother's absence didn't deter him from agreeing to help—just so long as Grace was there.

'If you hadn't asked, I couldn't have agreed.'

She blinked and peered closer at him.

'You'll do it?'

'Maybe.' Rik shot her a rueful grin.

'You understand Bas won't be there? It isn't an opportunity to meet your brother and talk to him.'

'You made that perfectly clear.' He dipped his head. 'But there's more than one way to get to know a person. The friends he chooses to keep can sometimes reveal a lot more about someone than anything anyone says about them.'

Grace's breath caught, and the impact was like a hot lick along his very sex.

'You mean me.'

'I do,' he murmured. 'People claim he's a rampant playboy, bouncing from one woman to the next and never ready to settle. But the fact that he has chosen you as his friend—the person I think he confides in—tells me a whole other story.'

'Is that right?' Her voice was deliciously husky. As if she was fighting back sinful thoughts.

Or was it more what he was doing?

'It is indeed.'

He was teetering so close to the edge of the rabbit hole here, where he wanted to simply sweep her up and throw her over his shoulder—caveman style—and carry her back to his private cave. Or, in his case, luxury hotel suite.

He might have had his fair share of partners in his life, but none of them had ever got under his skin the way that Grace had.

He needed to try to get the conversation back to a more level footing.

'So...' He paused. 'What exactly does this festival helping out entail?'

She blinked at him, her dark pupils taking a moment to adjust. He understood what she was feeling all too well.

She coughed briefly, to clear her throat. To regroup.

'Okay, so you'd be repairing some old booths, reviving others, and then manning a couple of stalls on festival week.'

'Bas repairs booths? Himself? He doesn't pay someone?'

'It's for charity, so everything we can do for free puts more money into the hands of those who need it.' Grace smiled at some memory that didn't include him, and he hated that his gut clenched so tightly.

'You've been doing this for a few years, then?' He forced himself to sound casual.

'Yeah, near enough ten years.' She sounded proud. 'Bas is quite the handyman when he wants to be, but don't worry if you're not so good. I can repair whilst you paint.'

She was teasing him, Rik realised. Tentatively, but teasing nonetheless. He found he rather liked it.

'I built my own house back in Sweden—I think I can help repair a few booths.'

'You built your own house?' Grace exclaimed.

He thought about the simple house, set in such a gloriously quiet location.

'It's more of a log cabin really, right in the Tyresta National Forest. It's a place to go if I want to escape modern life. No internet, no TV, limited mod cons.'

'It sounds isolating.' She didn't sound keen.

He didn't realise he'd moved until his hand reached out to brush a stray hair off her cheek.

'You make it sound like a bad thing,' he pointed out quietly. 'Are you that much of a city girl?'

'Through and through.' She nodded, though it didn't escape him how her breath caught. 'I make no apologies.'

'Where did you live before Thorncroft?' he asked abruptly. Not sure why.

Still, he wasn't surprised when that shuttered look slammed down over her features.

'Here and there.'

It shouldn't needle him so much that Grace

was so guarded with him. Yet it did. Somehow, he fought his way to easing the tone again.

'So—' he made himself sound cheerful '—you build and repair stalls for a charity fete?'

She raised one shoulder.

'I like the idea of giving back a little. And it's always for good causes.'

'And it's a tradition you do with my brother?'

'It is,' she affirmed. 'Does that surprise you?'

Rik didn't know why he thought about the question. He didn't need to.

'No. It doesn't,' he conceded after a few seconds.

How many times had he and his brother stopped to help someone after school? Whether it was collecting their prescriptions or running to the local shop for a bottle of milk, Bas had always been keen on helping people.

Why would he have grown up any different?

'I have a free day at the weekend,' she told him. 'How about then?'

He thought of his schedule, and his determination that this would be the weekend he finally made his brother talk to him.

Then he thought about spending the day with Grace.

And he told himself that it wasn't about spending time with Grace, so much as getting to know the person who seemed to know his brother best.

He wasn't sure he believed it.

'Okay.' He dipped his head in agreement. 'A day at the weekend seems fine.'

'You don't need to flannel me, Doc, I can take it.' The old man was clearly choking back tears as he stared through the glass of the isolation room to where his son lay.

Rik looked through the glass, too. He didn't need to see the clock on the wall to know that he was late for his painting date with Grace; he already knew that. But his patients came first— they always did.

But he figured she would understand. The more he worked with her, or people who had known her a while, the clearer picture he got of her.

She was quiet—not the kind to normally go having one-night stands—which shouldn't have made him feel as punch-drunk as it did. She was loyal to a fault, though, according to everyone, that loyalty was primary reserved for his brother. And she was committed to her job.

It just made him like her more. And though that should set alarms bells off in his head, Rik didn't hear a single warning sound.

'It isn't flannel,' Rik replied gently.

The old man made an odd *tsk*ing sound.

'I was a firefighter myself, and I've seen plenty of my guys with third-degree burns as extensive as this. I know the odds are against my kid.'

'Then you'll also know that medicine is improving year on year,' Rik continued. 'I deal with burns every day, and the study that I'm working on at the moment is showing a reduced mortality in full thickness or third-degree burns, from around forty-five per cent down to eight per cent when excise and grafting are carried out within the first three days of the initial injury.'

Slowly, the man twisted to look at Rik.

'You're talking about improving his survival odds from fifty-fifty to over ninety per cent?'

'If they're good surgical candidates, yes,' Rik confirmed. 'Your son is a good surgical candidate.'

For a long while, the man just stared through the window.

'He's all I've got,' he whispered, more to himself than to Rik.

Another moment of silence ticked by and then the man turned to him again.

'So what are the options?'

'There are two types of graft used to cover the wound bed,' Rik told him carefully. 'Skin replacement and skin substitute. The first is when we harvest healthy skin from the patient themselves, while the second—skin substitute—is a mixture of cells or tissues and includes biomaterial and engineered tissue.'

'You're talking about skin substitute for my son, then?' the older man said slowly. 'Looking at the extent of his burns, he doesn't have enough healthy skin for you to harvest for a graft.'

'Which is why I am recommending a split-thickness skin-graft approach. It only takes the epidermis and upper layer of dermis, and it means the same donor sites can be harvested after one or two weeks.'

'That still won't give you enough, though,' the old firefighter noted grimly. 'Will it?'

'Not as it is,' Rik agreed.

'Then…what?'

It was always a fine line, deciding how much of the finite detail of the procedure that his patients and their families needed to know. With a parent like this, who had no doubt seen more than his fair share of horrific injuries, and deaths, it was clear that the more information he could give, the better.

'Then we have a further option known as meshing graft. This is where we cut slits into the skin graft to enable it to stretch over more surface area. Sometimes as much as four times greater. A further benefit to this is that meshing can prevent seroma and haematoma formation beneath the graft. However, this method can result in significant scarring, tissue-tightening at the site, and an increased risk of infection.'

'But my boy could survive,' the man whispered.

'There is a greater chance, yes.'

There was another long silence as both men observed the young lad lying in the bed beyond the glass. Until the older man shook his head as though trying to free his thoughts.

'And what about the skin substitute? The engineered tissue?'

'The substitutes I'm looking at are biosynthetic products—skin regeneration templates that we can use to build a sort of scaffolding for the new skin. It will give a temporary wound coverage, which we would then have to remove before skin grafting.'

He was also considering an amniotic membrane graft as a short-term dressing. In any main hospitals, the cost of virus testing made it a prohibitive option. But wasn't that the beauty of being backed by someone like the Jansen Centre, with its almost unlimited resources.

The biggest potential hurdle he faced as a temporary member of the Jansen surgical team, however, was having to go to either Magnus or Bas for ultimate approval.

'And this will work?' the old man demanded suddenly. 'Really work?'

He was looking for assurance. A guarantee. Rik couldn't blame him—after all, it was his only son. But he had to be honest.

'As with anything, there is no one hundred per cent guarantee,' he said gently. 'And even if the skin grafts work, there will be a trade-off with cosmetic and functional outcomes. Burn scars can cause depression, pain, decreased range of motion, among others.'

'But he'll be alive, which is more than many of the guys I've worked with are.'

'Then I'll leave you to think,' Rik confirmed. 'In the meantime, my team will continue debriding the wound. He *is* in good hands.'

'And if I have more questions?'

'Then you can speak to anyone here, day or night,' Rik assured him. And that was the beauty of the Jansen Centre—there was always a liaison staff available, any time, to talk to the patient's family, and allay their fears, or to find someone who could. 'And either I or another member of my team will talk you through everything you need to know.'

With the final, discreet nod to the nurse at the station behind them, Rik headed out of the unit.

He was late.

He wasn't supposed to be working, he'd only called in to check on his patients before heading out to meet Grace for this stall-painting business. But seeing the man standing there like that, the old firefighter side of him warring with the grieving father side, he'd known he couldn't walk away. Not without talking to the man.

But he suspected that, of all people, Grace would fully understand that.

* * *

'You're late,' Grace observed casually as he walked through the door where they'd agreed to meet. 'I was beginning to think you'd changed your mind.'

He wondered if the idea had dismayed her at all. From her upbeat demeanour, one might have thought not. But there had been a moment there, when he'd first walked in, when he thought her eyes might have lit up. Just a little bit.

'I wanted to check on a couple of my patients and I ran into their family member, who needed answers,' he explained, pulling off his jacket and grabbing a paintbrush.

'Ah,' Grace acknowledged simply. As if it didn't matter either way. 'Anyway, take your pick. You said you were good with a saw.'

'Right.'

Rik suppressed a wry grin and glanced around the room obligingly. Huge pieces of wood and plastic, in various states of repair, were propped against the warehouse walls, whilst several eight-foot panels glistened already with fresh coats of paint.

Grace had clearly been busy.

'So, what's the plan?'

She cast him a long look, clearly expecting more comment. He merely waited patiently.

'See that panel over to your right? The next

one. Yes, that one. Can you start repairing it? Materials are on the other side of that wall.'

Away from her. He couldn't help but wonder if that was deliberate. Was she trying to keep some distance between them?

'Wouldn't it be easier if they were on hand around here? There's plenty of room.'

'There is now, yes.' The sober, serious look she assumed almost made him grin. 'But in a few weeks there'll be more of us here, things get cramped and the sawdust gets into the paint if we don't separate it all.'

He wasn't sure he liked the idea of more people in this space. He preferred the idea of being alone with Grace.

So much for telling himself that he was doing all this to get to better know the friend of his long-lost sibling, and not because he harboured any secret desire to actually get to know her better.

'Understood,' he replied impassively.

And she found she hated this closed-off side of Rik. The one where he kept her at arm's length. It made her think that he was more like his brother than either of them would care to admit.

'So, tell me about this cabin that you built,' she asked at last, hoping to draw him out.

To get back to the Rik who had made her feel... so feminine.

'What would you like to know?' he asked. His tone still deliberately even.

'Whatever you want to tell me.'

But he locked his jaw and looked distinctly underwhelmed.

'I can tell you that it isn't like this bright city. Though the hospital where I work is. Clearly not your scene.'

And she found herself bristling before she could stop herself.

'Maybe not so much my scene,' she bit out without meaning to. 'I was thinking about leaving this place anyway.'

She could pretend that she knew what she was doing, and that she'd dropped a crumb in order to get him to open up, too. But Grace didn't think that was what had happened.

She rather feared that she'd told him because she'd wanted him to know her better. Because she'd hoped he would understand.

'Leaving to go where?' he demanded, and some small victory shot through her that he looked so intent.

'Anywhere,' she answered truthfully. 'Everywhere.'

Because, before she'd felt compelled to return to Thorncroft, her childhood dream had been to travel. She'd spent half her formative years studying the books her parents had pushed her way, and half her time scouring geography books and planet guides, dreaming of the places she would visit when she was older.

And she didn't think she'd visited a single one of them.

'What about ties?' Rik asked curiously. 'Family, I mean.'

The question shouldn't scrape at her as it did. Grace forced another smile.

'Not really.'

He eyed her with interest.

'Sorry for your loss.'

But the way his regard caught hers made her feel more exposed than ever.

'They aren't dead,' she told him quietly. 'They're just…distant.'

He didn't answer, and she found herself talking some more. If only to fill the silence. Or that was what she told herself.

'They must be proud of you.'

'Of course,' she answered automatically.

Though the truth was that they weren't. That nothing had quite made them proud enough to forgive her the way she'd let them down as a teenager.

'So my brother has been the family you never had.'

That was one way of putting it.

'Does that surprise you?' Grace asked.

'Not really. It's more like the brother I remember. Kind. Empathetic. If there was a kid on their own, or getting bullied, Bas was always in there, pulling them into his gang. He would always stand up to the bullies.'

'And what about you?' she asked. 'I'm guessing you were the same.'

Rik laughed suddenly, making her jump.

'We might look similar now, but at six or seven, I weighed three stone wet through. Bas was more like a tank. Where he led, I followed. I might have stood beside him, if half a step back, but I never instigated.'

She frowned.

'I just can't see that. You're so...you. I can't see you standing on the sidelines, too scared to step forward.'

'I never said I was scared.' He flashed a devilish smile. 'But Bas was always the bold one, throwing himself into the fray. Looking before he leapt.'

Yes, she could see that. Rik, the cautious one. Quietly confident to his reactionary brother.

'Anyway, I should do some work.' He effectively shut the conversation down, that easily. And Grace let him.

Because chasing the hurricane that was Rik might be exhilarating, but it was also draining.

CHAPTER TEN

IT DIDN'T TAKE him long to decide the best course of action to effect a repair, and for half an hour he worked on the panel. The radio playing in the background eased the need for conversation, and Rik couldn't help smiling to himself when, after a while, Grace began humming to herself. Then singing.

A few old tracks that made him think of Mrs P, and the way she'd taught him and his brother to jive a little, when they'd been kids. Not that he remembered it now, of course.

But it was the sheer happiness, the freedom in her voice, that conjured up those unexpected memories and made him smile.

He was pretty sure she'd even forgotten he was there.

'You do this every year?'

Grace stopped singing, looking up at him in surprise.

'I do. I mean, I don't do it alone, there's a whole team of us, from the hospital and the wider community. Some of them work the booths on the day, and some paint or repair, and others might do both.'

'There's no one else here now, though,' Rik pointed out.

'You don't say?' Grace laughed. 'Give it an hour or so. It's still early but someone is bound to turn up. They would have had a group working last night when we were on shift.'

'And do you?' he asked curiously. 'Help out on the booths?'

'If I'm not working.' Grace nodded. 'For the last two years, I've worked the water-dunking stand with your brother. I just gather the sponges whilst he sits on the trap door above a glass water tank and people throw the sponges at a target.'

'Bas does?'

'Yep.' She nodded with a grin. 'He wears jeans, no top, and the queue is always incredibly long. It always raises an insane amount of money.'

'I thought he was Thorncroft's playboy surgeon.'

It didn't seem very playboy-like to him. And, from what little he'd heard about their father, he couldn't see Magnus liking it, either.

'It is for charity, after all.' She narrowed her eyes at him. 'You don't have to believe me, but you wanted to know more about your brother, and this is what he likes to do—help people. He also helps set up before the fete, man a booth during, and helps clear up after.'

'I wasn't mocking,' Rik told her.

If anything, it was more like the man he'd spent decades imagining his brother would have turned into. Before the ignored communications, and the Lothario reputation.

But Grace didn't know any of that, and Rik wasn't sure why he chose not to tell her.

'And what about you, *älskling*? What other things do you like to do?'

It was as if he'd asked her the theory of quantum mechanics, rather than make a simple enquiry into her personal life. After one beat seeped into the next, he told her as much.

Slowly, she lowered her paintbrush.

'Work doesn't leave a lot of time for hobbies.'

'You must have some?'

'Of course,' she agreed, but didn't elaborate until the silence between them seemed to demand it. 'I like…going for runs. And reading. Sometimes, I like ice skating when they bring a small rink into the city centre at Christmas time.'

'Is that it?' he challenged, and he didn't know why he was pressing the matter.

Perhaps because a part of him sensed she was keeping something back from him, and it bothered him. Far more than he thought it had a right to.

'As I said, I don't really have time for hobbies.' She winced.

'Not even dancing?' he demanded, deliberately lightening his tone as he strode across the room and cranked the music up.

'What are you doing?' She clutched her paint-brush tighter.

'The night of the gala you clearly knew how to dance. Just ballroom, or do you know a little jive?'

'Why?'

'Such suspicion.' He grinned. 'Though I note you aren't denying it.'

'Because I don't see what dancing has to do with painting these booths.'

'It doesn't,' agreed Rik. 'But when my brother and I were kids, we had a cook for a while. And she taught us how to jive, and lindy hop.'

'How…nice.' Grace wrinkled her nose. But that quirk of her lips gave her away.

'I rather think I'd like to try again now,' he told her.

'You're asking me to dance?'

'No. I've forgotten how to do any of it,' Rik confessed. 'I'm asking you to teach me.'

'I don't think—'

'Not a lot,' he cut her off. 'Just a little. Just for a bit of fun.'

She was clearly tempted—though he wondered how he could read her so easily.

'Here?' she asked, eventually.

'Why not? There's plenty of room.' He extended his arms and turned. 'Where better than a vast warehouse?'

'A dance hall?' she asked wryly.

'I don't know any dance halls around here.' He laughed. 'Do you?'

'Only Miss Beverley's. It's where I learned ballet and tap as a kid, before my parents decided that was too frivolous.'

Grace clamped her mouth shut instantly, her cheeks colouring as she realised her mistake. He could have let it go—it was clear she wished she hadn't forgotten herself.

But he couldn't. Some inexplicable desire to understand her better coursed through him.

'When you were a kid?'

'Forget I said anything,' she clipped out, trying to back away but hitting the wall behind them.

Swiftly, he followed, placing his hands on the wall either side of her. Effectively caging her without ever laying a finger on her. Though she could have ducked away, had she really wanted to.

Rik thought it spoke volumes that she didn't.

'You told me you met my brother at university? That you only moved here to Thorncroft to complete you career training?'

'I did…sort of.' Grace sucked in a breath, her eyes glittering with emotions he couldn't read as she stared up at him. 'The truth is, I was born here.'

'In this county?'

'In this city. In Thorncroft Royal Infirmary, to be exact.'

'Then why the big secret? Why pretend you only moved here in your twenties?'

'Because no one knows.' She lifted her shoulders lightly, as if it were no big deal. Her tense body language told a different story. 'We left when I was sixteen. My parents got offered jobs at a university in a different city, so we moved. I always wanted to return.'

'Do you have family here?'

Grace blinked at him for a moment.

'My grandparents are dead, and I was an only child, like my father. My aunt lives in Australia, though she and mother were never really close anyway.'

Which sounded like a denial but, Rik couldn't help but notice, wasn't quite one.

'So when my brother suggested moving to Thorncroft to complete your residencies…?'

'I joined him because it felt like more than just a coincidence that the world-renowned Jansen Suite should be based here. That it was *fate* somehow telling me it was time to return.'

'Why?'

This time, she jerked her chin up and glowered at him.

'It doesn't really matter.'

They both knew that she was lying, but clearly she'd said all she was going to say.

He had to think that it would have to be enough. For now.

'You don't have to talk about it.' Rik pushed off the wall without warning and took a step away.

He didn't think it was his imagination that her hand twitched—as though she'd been going to reach for him.

As though she felt too exposed to be left there alone.

'It's been pleasant so far. I don't want to ruin it by prying into your personal life.'

Except, inexplicably, that was exactly what he wanted to do.

He wanted to know this woman. To understand her. Yet she was supposed to be simply a pleasant diversion from the main business of being here, so it didn't make any sense at all.

'I promise I won't ask anything more. Wait, this is a good track.'

Moving quickly over to increase the volume on the radio, Rik strode back and held his hand back out to her, gratified when she took it with only the briefest hesitation. But the mood had started to lift in the room. Just as he'd intended.

'Okay.' He grinned. 'Let's see how good a teacher you are. Then, if I can hold my own, I might let you take me to a dance.'

'How lovely for me,' Grace remarked dryly. Then laughed, as though in spite of herself.

The sweet sound glided over him like a silken hand—just as it had that first night together. He'd missed that laugh, though he hadn't realised how much until now.

They danced through several good songs, with Rik quite surprised at how quickly Mrs P's lessons came back to him. He lacked the surprisingly easy fluidity of Grace's movements, but he felt pleased that he'd held his own.

Especially because it seemed to have restored some of the effortless banter between the two of them.

But, in many ways, the revelation had raised more questions than it had answered. And he could pretend that getting to know Grace was about getting to know his brother all he liked. The truth was that, with Grace around, it was getting harder and harder to remember why he'd come here in the first place.

'This was more fun than I remembered,' he told her, after the last song finished. 'I think we ought to discuss other potential hobbies that may interest you.'

'Is that so?' Grace asked, grabbing her bottle of water before collapsing onto a stool.

She drank deeply, then offered the bottle to him.

'Thanks.' He took a couple of quick swigs. 'Over dinner tomorrow, I think. Somewhere nice and exclusive. I'll pick you up at seven-thirty.'

And he liked it rather too much that Grace didn't even attempt to object.

* * *

Grace stared up at the restaurant frontage and tried not to gawk.

The Cherry Icing was one of the city's finest restaurants. Its waiting list was famously months long.

'We aren't eating here, surely?'

Rik had only invited her out the day before. She was fairly certain that even the Jansen name couldn't have gained entrance that quickly.

'Bad choice?' Rik grinned wryly. 'I was told it's a dining experience not to be missed.'

'Definitely not to be missed. But how did you even manage it?'

'Turns out I operated on the patron's son when I first arrived here. The kid is sous chef here, and he'd had an accident—cycling accident, not kitchen related, I might add. Still, the fear was that he would have to have his hand amputated.'

'How awful.'

'Not to brag—' he grinned '—I managed to not only save it, but restore almost full use.'

'So modest,' she couldn't help but tease him.

Surely it should worry her more, how easy things always seemed to be between them?

'Indeed.' Rik's grin broadened. 'Anyway, my patient's father was so grateful that he made me promise to visit the restaurant while I was in the city, and assured me I could count on a table whenever I wanted it. I called him last night, and he was as good as his word.'

And he'd used his invitation for her. Grace felt ridiculously special.

Taking her arm to escort her in, Rik leaned down to murmur in her ear, his hot breath tickling her neck and sending her pulse spinning off erratically.

'Just promise me one thing.'

Grace flicked her tongue out over her suddenly dry lips.

'What's that?'

'That you'll enjoy the meal, and not just order salad only to push it around the plate.'

She twisted her neck around so fast that it almost stung.

'If I hadn't spent the past five years dreaming of eating here, I think I should take offence at that.'

'Then I apologise.' Rik laughed.

That low, rich sound that always rumbled through her so deliciously, and made her wish that things between them were different.

Wish that they were *more*.

His laugh always made her forget she was supposed to be keeping a close eye on Rik, and then reporting back, when all she really wanted to do was enjoy whatever time she could snatch with this intelligent, caring, sexy-as-hell Viking.

And then, as he removed her coat for her and

handed it off, the look of frank appreciation in his gaze made her forget everything all over again.

He leaned into her, his lips brushing the side of her head tantalisingly.

'I also should apologise for not telling you how incredible you look tonight.'

She valiantly tried to supress the delicious shiver that tripped its way over her, but by the curl of lips against her skin, Grace didn't think she'd succeeded.

'Thank you,' she murmured. 'You don't look so bad yourself.'

And then his palm settled on the small of her back as they followed the maître d' through the tables and to their own, and she felt all the more cherished, and sensual. Like the kind of effortlessly sexy woman that no man had ever made her feel like before.

It almost made her feel bereft when they reached their table and sat down—the contact lost. *Almost.* The exquisiteness of the restaurant just about made up for it.

Grace took a few discreet looks around and exhaled softly to herself.

'I've never been here before,' she confessed, running her hand along the impossibly smooth burr oak surface of their table.

'I'm pleasantly surprised,' Rik confessed. 'I thought you might have been here before. Look up.'

Dutifully, she did, gasping at the sight.

'It's one of the earlier examples of Italianate Renaissance architecture.' Rik leaned in once again, his head close to hers so that he could point out the tiny features that she might otherwise have missed. 'Possibly based on some of the work of the architect, Inigo Jones, in London.'

'I never even knew.' She shook her head. 'The reviews I've heard always seem to focus on the food, not the atmosphere.'

'Here, you have both. Jones, like many of the educated men of the sixteenth century, travelled quite extensively, including to places like Rome. It is said he particularly admired the work of the architect Andrea Palladio.'

'How do you know all this?' Grace turned to look at him.

It seemed the more she learned about the man, the more there was to learn. A whole lifetime, perhaps?

The thought startled her.

'It interests me.' He waved a hand almost dismissively. 'Call it a bit of a hobby. But at one time, I did consider becoming an architect.'

'What made you change your mind?' she asked, genuinely curious.

He didn't answer immediately, but peered at her intently. As if trying to decide how much to share. But before he could decide, they were interrupted by their waiter, and the moment was lost.

'So…' Rik reclined in his seat in that casual

way of his that seemed to highlight every bit of his masculinity. 'Other than your work, and volunteering to repaint old booths for charity fetes, what do you like to do, Grace Henley?'

'Other than the two things that seem to take up fourteen or fifteen hours of most days?' She laughed. 'Not a lot.'

'What did you used to do, then?' He wasn't deterred. 'Before your life got so full?'

'Is it full?'

Grace stopped abruptly as she heard the words that she hadn't intended to say. Hadn't even thought. No wonder Rik was watching her curiously.

And even though the voice in her head was commanding her to retrace her steps, when she opened her mouth, she heard herself continuing.

'I don't think my life has ever been what I thought it might be,' she confessed. 'Which isn't to say that I don't like being a doctor, because I do. If I'm honest, it's the only part of my life that I'm sure about. But when I was a kid, I used to dream of so much more.'

'Such as,' he prompted softly when she fell silent.

And she lifted her shoulders to shrug the question off but, once again, she heard her own voice speaking the words she hadn't even allowed herself to think.

'I used to dream of going places, of seeing

things. Not just through books, but with my own eyes. I don't know.' She glanced up at the ceiling. 'I wanted to visit Florence. I imagined going to the pyramids in Egypt. I wanted to stand in front of the Taj Mahal.'

She stopped abruptly, feeling foolish.

'That sounds silly. I'm sorry.'

'It doesn't sound remotely silly.' Rik frowned. 'So, why didn't you?'

And it was on the tip of Grace's tongue to tell him the truth. To confess the story that she had never told another living soul.

The reason why she'd felt so compelled to return to this place. The connection that was probably imagined but meant that she couldn't leave. The uncertainty that meant she hadn't really been able to move on with her life, in more than a decade.

She caught herself just in time.

'My job is here in Thorncroft.' She tried to sound casual but failed, even to her own ears.

'You can be an obstetrician anywhere,' Rik pointed out.

And Grace knew there was no answer to that. None that would make any sense to this man, anyway. But then, as the silence began to bulge and press between them, he rescued her.

Just as he'd done in the warehouse yesterday afternoon.

'Well, I've travelled to those places, and done

those things, so I can tell you that if it's what you want to do, then do it. We each only have one life, and it's worth going, and seeing, and experiencing, as much as you possibly can.'

'I thought you preferred simpler things. The simple life?' she asked, fighting to get her hand back into the conversation. 'Didn't you say you'd built a log cabin?'

Rik looked surprised by her question.

'I did. But you don't want to know about that.'

'I do.' She lifted one shoulder elegantly. 'You made it sound like a nice place to get away.'

'It's quiet. Not like the cities. You said you were a city girl.'

'I realise that.' She hesitated. 'And it's true, I used to love the city, with its bright lights and nightlife. There's always something to do, somewhere that's open.'

'But…?' he prompted, when she stopped.

'I don't know.' She gave a half-laugh. 'It doesn't feel like…*me*. It hasn't for almost a year now.'

'So, change it.'

'I am changing it.' She snapped her eyes up to his. 'Or, at least, I was changing it. I was getting ready to make a move a few months ago, but then…'

She tailed off and Rik didn't speak, but she felt the weight of his gaze on her as she toyed with the stem of her wine glass.

'Anyway, where did you say it was? In a national forest?'

Rik almost didn't answer. She got the impression that the cabin was his private bolt-hole and he never shared it with anyone. Apparently, not really even in conversation.

But then, just as she was about to take a sip of wine and try to change the topic, he started speaking.

'It's on the edge of the Tyresta National Park. About a twenty-mile drive from Stockholm.'

Did she dare ask more? She certainly wanted to know what it was about it that had so captivated him.

'How did you end up with it?'

He peered at her, as though assessing her motives. But she didn't know what she should say, so she stayed silent.

'I'd run into another obstacle in my search for my brother,' he confessed, unexpectedly. 'I started lurching from one surgery to another, probably just to try to regain some kind of control, I suppose. Anyway, I was treating one patient who told me that he and his wife had always wanted to go on a round-the-world trip, but they'd always put it off because of time, or money, or family.'

'Sounds like me.' She laughed, but it was a shaky sound.

She wondered if he could read how much she

was beginning to find this place—even the hospital—was suffocating her.

'My patient told me that if he recovered, he intended to sell a rare plot of land that his family had owned for almost one hundred years, and they would go. So, I made him a deal. If I healed him, I'd buy the land.'

'It was that simple?' She sounded incredulous, and Rik smiled.

'It was that simple. I bought the land on the Thursday, I headed down there on the Friday and camped overnight in the forest, and by the time I was back on shift on the Sunday I'd already started drawing up plans for a home.'

'So what's it like in this forest of yours?'

He looked at her, met her eye.

'It's incomparable,' he told her quietly. 'A stunning landscape, sculpted by the hand of the Ice Age itself, with a coniferous forest boasting ancient, giant trees as old as four hundred years.'

She was enthralled. The look in his expression drawing her in as much as his words. Painting a picture so vivid that she thought she might truly be standing there, right now. It was so utterly enticing.

'Also, unlike the ice rink you love that gets transported into the city at Christmas time,' he reminded her of their previous conversation, 'there are lakes in the park on which you can skate all winter long.'

And Grace couldn't decide whether it was the idea of the cabin or the man that bewitched her the most.

CHAPTER ELEVEN

'I HAD NO idea the fete was going to be quite like this,' Rik marvelled, even before the pair of them stepped onto the field.

There was a variety of rides, from mini roller coasters to spinning teacups, a huge inflatable slide that had to be about thirty feet high, with a vertiginous set of covered steps leading to the top, and a plethora of different booths and stalls. Many of which she assumed he recognised from their many painting sessions over the past month.

At least he'd finally got to meet the rest of the charity board team, even if the ever-more-crowded warehouse *had* put a stop to their impromptu jive dancing.

'Infectious, isn't it?' Grace grinned as she soaked up the buzz of the carnival atmosphere.

She didn't think it was her imagination that everything was injected with that much more joy whenever Rik was around.

'I have to admit that, even having seen all those panels in that warehouse, I thought it would be a few stalls in the car park. I had no idea it would be such an extravaganza.'

Rik glanced over the multitude of booths, carnival rides, and bandstands filling up the local fields behind Thorncroft Royal, and she chuckled merrily.

'It was a bit like that when I was a kid,' Grace confessed. 'But now it's a big event, and it seems to get bigger every year. This year we've got a new bungee-trampoline thing that I think I'll be too terrified to try.'

'I can't imagine you being terrified of anything.'

His voice was even, yet he watched her for one long moment. As if there was something about her that he was trying to work out. As if she… mattered, to him.

She shook the foolish notion from her head and injected a deliberately cheery tone to her voice.

'Well, I can only say that I think I'll be sticking to hooking a duck or throwing a dart at a balloon wall.'

'Will that be before the dunking stall, or after?'

'After.' Grace danced gleefully. She couldn't seem to help herself. 'We don't open that until it's warmer, say around lunchtime?'

'Is that so?' Rik grinned, making her stomach flip-flop. 'Then, is there anything I can do?'

'Face painting.'

'Sorry?'

She didn't even try to conceal her amusement.

'We're going to do some face painting.' She led him to the stall and took over from the two colleagues who looked more than ready for a break.

The line of kids snaked around quite a way.

'Okay, first take your sponge and get some of the white face paint, like this. Good. Right.'

Rik's altogether serious expression made Grace grin.

'Now, you're going to paint the face white down the nose, see? And around the mouth, here? Great, and finally sponge in two tiger ears above his eyebrows, like so.'

She leaned back critically to inspect her work, and Rik's. She had to admit, his looked pretty good. Too good for a beginner.

She eyed him suspiciously, not trusting his innocent look for a second.

'Have you done this before?'

'I have not.' He grinned. 'But it's face painting, *älskling*. Not surgery.'

'Tell that to the kid whose tiger face you mess up,' she warned good-naturedly.

'Point taken. Now what?'

If it hadn't been for the little ears around them, she might have said something different.

'Now, load up your sponge with some yellow. Okay, here we go.'

They worked together for about fifteen minutes, with Grace working slowly to give him time to copy.

By the end, it actually looked like the tiger it was meant to be, and Rik leaned back to admire his handiwork just as Grace sent the kid off with a lollipop as a reward for his patience.

'Okay, I know I said you needed to be accurate, but it isn't a gallery opening at the V&A, you know.' She laughed. 'Turn around and look at the line.'

Obediently, Rik turned. The queue was already beginning to snake around the corner.

'Speed up, slow coach,' she told him, winking at the child seated at her table and making them giggle. 'We have a lot to get through before you have to get ready for your dunking.'

And she laughed at Rik's muttered response as they both concentrated on their new roles for the next few hours.

'Are you hungry?' she asked as a couple more colleagues came over to relieve them of their face-painting duties.

With a final flourish, Rik dropped his brush into the cleaning tub.

'Famished. What time is it?'

'Nearly lunch time. We get an hour free, and then it's time for you to delight the crowd with your shirtless dunking.'

'I can't wait.' He grimaced as his stomach gave a loud grumble of concurrence. 'Where do you suggest eating, then?'

'There are a couple of good food trucks.'

Rik glanced around sceptically.

'I think not.'

'Snob.' She laughed before she could help herself. 'There's nothing wrong with eating here.'

'I beg to differ.'

'Come on.' She elbowed him playfully in the ribs before she realised what she was doing. 'Live dangerously.'

She felt the weight of his gaze on her, but she refused to turn around. Had she just ruined the easy repartee between them?

She certainly hoped not.

After a long moment, to her relief, Rik let out a dramatic groan.

'All right, then, you've convinced me. Which one do you suggest?'

She was pretty sure she already knew, but she turned a complete three-sixty all the same, taking in all the trucks.

'Xavier's Home-Cooked Chilli,' she declared.

'Xavier's it is,' Rik agreed as they headed over to the mobile kitchen together. The place was pristine, but then it had to be, catering to a hospital of medical professionals and their families.

Still, it didn't take long for their food to come to them, complete with little wedges of lime and a swirl of soured cream.

They strolled across to where a collection of tables had been set out, and sat down, with her on a chair whilst Rik straddled the bench.

'This,' Rik exclaimed, after the first mouthful, 'is truly incredible.'

Grace closed her eyes and savoured the taste.

'It is,' she agreed after a moment. 'And just think, if I'd left you to be a snob, you would have missed out completely.'

And there she was, teasing him again. As if it was the most natural thing in the world.

'Lesson learned.'

For a few minutes, all they did was eat, the rush and hassle of the day ebbing away as peace fell, and their growling bellies began to feel a little fuller.

'You know, I think I'm going to have to get this recipe and try it for myself some time.'

Grace eyed him for a moment, unaware of the words gathering on her tongue until she heard them spill out.

'Do you cook?'

Rik's head turned slowly, so slowly, to look at her again. For a moment, she wasn't even sure that he was going to answer.

'I do.'

Without warning, the weight of it struck her.

'So does your brother,' she said. 'Incredibly well, in fact. I'm guessing it's the cook you mentioned. The one who taught you to dance?'

She watched his jaw lock tight. And the harsh tic of his pulse. Then, somehow, he loosened it off again.

'Yes.'

'She taught you as seven-year-olds?'

It had to be before those awful events Bas had told her about had happened.

Another long silence.

'Sort of. We moved away from her just before our seventh birthday. But, yes, she'd been there all our lives up until then.'

'And she taught you both how to cook?'

'She taught us how to bake at first. Fun fairy cakes. Then, when she realised what home life was like, and how sometimes we wouldn't get anything to eat at night, she taught us how to make basic meals. I guess that must have given both of us a love of cooking. My brother really enjoys it, too?'

'He's always conjuring up mouth-watering stuff,' she managed, but she still caught up on the other thing he'd said.

'What do you mean, you didn't get to eat?'

But Rik ignored that part. It clearly wasn't a memory he wanted to revisit, but she thought she understood well enough.

'Mrs P taught us more than just how to cook. She taught us how to be good men. She taught us what was right. What is it that Aristotle said? Give me the boy until he is seven, and I will show you the man. Mrs P made us into the men we are today. At least, the better part of the men we are today.'

'I… I didn't know,' Grace admitted quietly.

'My brother never mentioned her?'

'Maybe he forgot about her?' she suggested tentatively. 'After all, he was only seven.'

'No.' There was no heat in the denial, more a quiet, grim certainty. And...something else. Something Grace thought looked a lot like a kind of anguish. 'He couldn't have forgotten about Mrs P. He couldn't have forgotten exactly what happened with her. With us. With our mother. It would make everything we went through...meaningless.'

She couldn't stop herself. Reaching forward, she touched her fingers to Rik's.

'If you're suggesting that Mrs P was part of the reason Bas ended up getting sent away, perhaps it's better that he's forgotten. Or, at least, buried it.'

'That's precisely why he needs to remember.' Rik eyed her again, his penetrating gaze locking with hers. 'I don't understand why he blames me for what happened. Or why he has chosen to forget Mrs P or her husband. But you need to help him.'

'I can't.'

'You have to. But you need to help him find the real truth.'

'He won't really listen to me any more.' She shook her head.

If he ever really had.

They'd been friends, but she'd listened to him more than he'd listened to her. Besides, Grace wasn't sure why, but she got the impression that Naomi stood more of a chance than anyone of making Bas listen.

They stopped talking, just giving themselves some time to sit and eat in peace.

But, surprisingly, it was more of a companionable stillness than an awkward silence. It was odd, but this...*thing* she had with Rik was closer than she'd ever been with her friend.

But in a matter of weeks, Rik would be gone. His stint on the exchange programme would be over and he would fly back to Sweden.

The prospect made Grace's stomach actually churn, and it took all she had to drag her mind back to nicer things.

Back to the idea of a water-drenched Rik, barefoot and shirtless, and his dark denim jeans soaked through and clinging lovingly to the legs she knew first hand to be sculptured masterpieces. Never mind her stomach, the mere thought of it was enough to set other body parts racing.

This was so *not* what she was supposed to be doing. But the truth was that she'd abandoned her original task of keeping an eye on him a while ago.

Probably from that first moment in the warehouse when they'd started dancing instead of painting.

Laughing, and having fun, as though they were a real couple. Or, if not that, then at least two people who were genuinely attracted to each other without any other agenda.

She'd stopped thinking about it because she hadn't wanted whatever they might have to be tainted any more. Now all she had to do was find a way to explain everything to Rik without telling him exactly what was going on with his brother and the baby.

Because, however else she might feel, that part of the story wasn't hers to tell.

Giving herself a mental shake, Grace dropped her fork into a near-empty bowl and cast Rik a wicked grin.

His dark gaze was her reward.

'Hurry up, I want to try my hand at the skittle wall and win a squeaky toy for Cooper. And then, we've got an afternoon on the water-dunking booth to look forward to.'

'Don't remind me.' He laughed, though she sensed that it was a little forced.

As if he was trying as hard as she was to get back to the breeziness of earlier. As if, like her, he didn't want to waste the rest of the short time they had left on things that didn't make them laugh.

And, abruptly, Grace wondered what she was holding back for. If there were only a few weeks before Rik left, how could she get hurt if she indulged just a little bit more?

What would happen if she threw caution to the

wind with Rik, and indulged in the less uptight side of herself? Just this once.

Grace sank into the soft leather seat of the back of the limousine taxi—one of a number reserved exclusively for the VIPs of the Jansen Suite—and closed her eyes in bliss as Rik slid in beside her. His hair was still wet from the dunking, but his change of clothes mercifully dry.

'Better?' he asked as he pulled the door closed on them, cocooning them in the darkness.

'Everything hurts,' she complained with a laugh. 'My feet, from racing around retrieving wet sponges, my hands from punching tickets, and my head, from all the screaming and laughter.'

'I seem to recall you were doing plenty of laughing,' he accused, with raised eyebrows. 'Every time that sponge hit the target and that trapdoor opened beneath me.'

Grace pulled her mouth into a tight line to keep from laughing again, as her deep blue eyes held his—so long that he could feel himself falling back under her spell.

But he shouldn't. He *mustn't*.

'Don't you know that actions have consequences, *älskling*?' Rik murmured, laughing when her eyes widened. Darkened.

'What consequences?'

'Allow me to show you.'

Before he could stop himself, or even think, he pulled her across the seats until she was sprawled across his knee, and his mouth was crushing hers.

Claiming her.

The way he'd been dreaming of doing all day.

All month.

A part of him might have expected Grace to fight him. If only for a moment, and if only for show. But she didn't even pretend that much. She simply collapsed against him, her chest pressed to his, and her arms looping around his head as if being with him was the only place she wanted to be.

'That's good,' she murmured. 'Because I think I have a few consequences of my own, given the way you kept deliberately splashing me every time.'

'Is that so, *älskling*?' he demanded.

And when she nodded, she kept her forehead pressed to his. Her mouth curved up in happiness.

'Oh, yes,' she told him. 'That's definitely so. A few lessons to be taught, I think. And they may take quite some time.'

And Rik forgot his promise to himself. He forgot who she was. He even forgot that they were in the back of a damned car. The need for her pounded through him, like a secret that he'd tried to lock away for too long now.

He was happy to tell himself that what he was doing now was nothing more than indulging in a last bit of fun before he returned home in a few weeks. He would happily stomp on any voice in his head snidely suggesting otherwise. But deep down, a different truth began to snake, and move.

But he could deal with that another day. For now, he just wanted to lose himself in the woman currently shifting on his lap. Meeting his kiss head-on, twisting herself around so that she was suddenly straddling him and he was no longer sure which one of them was teaching consequences to the other.

Worse, he didn't even care. So long as it never stopped.

She slid her fingers into his hair, pressing her body so tightly against his, as if she couldn't bear for there to be even a millimetre of space between them, making Rik groan. No matter that his mouth was still fused to hers. And no matter that he could feel the replying shiver work its way through her body as she rocked against the hardest part of him.

He had never willed a car-ride away so badly.

By the time they arrived at the hospital site—neither seeming to care that the limousine deposited them right outside the main entrance of the Garden Complex—it was all either of them could do to tumble out, thank the driver, and make their way up to Rik's rooms.

And then they were stumbling inside—a perfect echo of that first night together in the hotel suite. Only here, he had a suite of rooms, all bigger, and higher, and furnished even more luxuriously than the hotel.

Not that he cared about any of that, especially at this moment, save for the fact that he didn't think they would even make it to the bedroom. Already, their clothes were off in a shocking economy of movement, and they had barely made it into the elegant sitting room. If he didn't manage to take control they were going to be doing it down there, on the cold, hard solid wood floor.

Without warning, Rik scooped her up into his arms, and carried her directly to the bedroom. Taking matters, quite literally, into his own hands.

'You'd better hold on, *älskling*,' he muttered, depositing her onto the large bed.

But as he joined her he wondered which of them needed to hold on the most. Especially when he lay on his back, hauling her back to him to straddle him once again—the position that allowed him to see every inch of her delectable body. And every slick, perfect slide in and out of her.

She was never going to get enough of Rik, Grace thought some time later as he carried her exhausted, tingling body into the shower room and the to-die-for walk-in shower.

If she'd thought what had happened between them that first night—the night of the gala—

had been spectacular, then she had no words to describe what had just happened now. Because somehow, impossibly, it had been even better.

She could still taste him on her tongue. That generous gift of satin-wrapped steel. And she could still picture the look on his face when she'd first pushed him backwards to drop kisses down that solid wall of his chest, used her fingers to toy with the smattering of hair on his chest, and taken her tongue to the mouth-wateringly defined V-lines where his obliques met his lower abdominals.

And then, that moment of power that had jolted through her as she'd lowered her head to take him in her mouth—her eyes not once leaving his—whilst his breathing had changed in an instant. A ragged, rapid sound that had guided her, and thrilled her, all at once.

God, how she'd enjoyed that. Thrilling him and celebrating him at the same time. Taking him deep into the heat of her mouth, sucking on him, then sliding him out to let the cool air dance over his tip before flicking her tongue over him.

She knew she would remember those deep, guttural noises for ever. So utterly carnal, making her feel as though she held every inch of control in the situation. It was a heady experience.

Still, she hadn't been entirely surprised when he hadn't let her finish. Not the way she'd wanted to, anyway. Not in any way that would have meant him giving up control completely.

Because he hadn't wanted to with her? Or because he couldn't bring himself to do that with anyone?

Grace found she couldn't bear the idea that he still didn't quite trust her.

'Are you joining me?'

She turned abruptly as Rik's voice floated to her in the air. The sound of the shower cascading down like some glorious waterfall, the steam filling up the room. And when he reached for her, she didn't hesitate for a moment, allowing him to pull her gently under the blissful flow and revelling in the way his soaped-up hands sought out her body again.

As if they didn't have a care in the world.

'Do you need me to?' she teased hoarsely.

With a smile, Rik slid his arms around her, their naked bodies moving slickly against each other. It caused a delicious kind of friction.

'I just might.' He sounded raw. Half undone already.

Just the way that she felt, too. She leant back on the glass—already warmed by the water—and pulled him with her.

'Show me,' she commanded.

And loved that he dutifully obeyed.

CHAPTER TWELVE

GRACE STOOD ON the balcony of Rik's hotel suite, gazing down at the twinkling lights of Thorncroft spread out before her. The air was damp, and it had been raining all evening, but even that hadn't been able to dampen her soaring spirits.

It had been creeping up on her ever since that night at the gala when she'd first met Rik—slowly at first, so that she hadn't noticed it, but now the feeling was so intense that she couldn't deny it.

She was happy. Not just happy—blissfully happy. So happy that she could actually feel it, like a warmth heating her from the inside out.

And it was Rik who had done that. The last two months had been like nothing she'd ever imagined. He'd helped her to shake off the fusty idea of love that she'd learned from her parents, and he'd shown her something so intense, and incredible.

Even better, she was beginning to realise that she might have done the same thing for him. The only proverbial fly in the ointment was that dark, niggling secret she desperately, terrifyingly, wanted to tell him.

Because how could this thing between them be real if she couldn't even tell him about the one event in her life that had shaped her the most?

'Come back to bed.'

Grace heard Rik stir behind her, and even as her heart leapt into her mouth a delicious trail of goosebumps raced over her skin.

'Join me,' she murmured softly, almost hoarsely. 'You have quite the view from up here.'

There was a brief pause, and then she heard him slide out of bed and into a pair of trousers that she knew without needing to see would be low-slung over his sculpted hips.

As he padded across the room towards her, she steadfastly kept her head to the city lights below, lest she lose her nerve.

'Beautiful, isn't it?'

'Stunning,' Rik agreed, and she knew he was looking at her rather than the view.

It would have been so easy to swallow her words. And her courage.

Grace wasn't sure how she managed not to. But she needed to tell him the truth. Some deep need was driving within her, willing her to finally tell someone. No, not just *someone*. Rather, to tell *Rik*.

Though she had no idea how to even begin. Grace opened her mouth, hoping to find the words to ease into it.

'My daughter is down there,' she blurted out instead. 'Somewhere.'

The words she'd never spoken aloud in her life, except for that one night. They rolled oddly around her tongue.

'Pardon?'

'I mean. Maybe.' She was losing her nerve now. 'I'd like to think so, anyway.'

The silence was almost unbearable. Grace had no idea how long she waited for Rik to reply. A lifetime, perhaps? Maybe two?

And then, at last…

'You have a daughter?'

It sounded so…*real* coming from him.

'I do,' Grace managed, suddenly feeling awe-struck.

'You have a baby? You? The most level-headed, career-orientated person I've met since I've been here?'

Her eyes pricked and heated unexpectedly.

'You have to stop putting me on this damned pedestal,' she burst out, not even aware she'd been so close to the brink until she heard her own voice bouncing back at her, off the balcony walls, and the cool, inky night sky beyond. 'I'm not this perfect person.'

He advanced on her, putting his hands on her shoulders in a gesture that she knew he intended as soothing.

'You're the most perfect person I've ever met,' he told her solemnly.

It should have been romantic.

Inspiring.

Instead, she clutched at her chest as though she could somehow rip off the tight, invisible cloak that felt as though it were suffocating her.

'No.' She jerked her head from side to side. 'I'm not. And it's too much. The pressure of it is too much.'

'There's no pressure.'

'There feels like pressure,' she countered.

'Why?'

'I don't know,' she cried, though quieter, this time. 'I'm not perfect, and shiny, and all the things you seem to think I am.'

'When have I told you that?' Rik demanded softly.

But her agitation was too far gone to rein in so easily.

'I can't be the person you look to as the epitome of all that is right and good, because that's not me. I'm every bit as flawed, and damaged, and broken as you. Just for different reasons.'

And she knew these were all her own fears, finally escaping after years of her stuffing them down, but that didn't seem to make it any easier to bear.

'You don't have to tell me this,' he assured her. 'If you don't want to.'

'I do.' She nodded vigorously, even as she still couldn't find the courage to turn and look at him. 'I've never told anyone this before. *Ever.* But I need to tell you now.'

Another tenuous moment pulled taut in her chest.

'Say as much or as little as you need,' Rik re-assured her.

And, somehow, it was the nudge she needed.

'I *had* a baby,' Grace managed, slowly at first. 'A long time ago. But she'll be fourteen now.'

And then she stopped, as if uncertain how to continue.

'And she's somewhere down there?' Rik prompted just as she thought she might flounder.

Grace grasped the lifeline gratefully.

'Yes,' then, 'no. Well…maybe.'

'Maybe?'

For another impossibly long moment, Grace felt Rik's stare bolting her down. She saw her own knuckles turn white on the railing. And she wondered if her legs were going to start swaying and collapsing beneath her.

But whatever she might have expected, it hadn't been for Rik to begin piecing it together so quickly. Faster than she could even begin to explain.

'This was the event that happened when you were sixteen,' he said. A statement, not a question, though his tone was carefully neutral. Non-judgemental. 'The reason that your family left Thorncroft.'

'It was.' Her throat felt suddenly parched.

'And this is the reason you came back here a decade ago.' It was impressive, just how easily he was working things through. 'This was what you meant by feeling it was *fate* when my brother suggested both of you should continue your training here. You came back for your daughter.'

'I did.'

It felt unimaginably good to finally be able to admit that aloud, after all this time. Grace felt a sob make its way through her chest, but she fought it back.

'Yet you haven't met her?'

The elation dulled in an instant. It took her a few attempts to work her mouth again.

'I haven't.' The words felt like glass paper, abrading her throat, her mouth, her ears. 'The truth is, when I say she's down there somewhere, I don't actually know if she is. I might have passed her on the street out there. Or she might live halfway around the world by now.'

'You didn't want to know?' Rik asked, and a kind of stillness settled over her.

'I was never allowed to.'

'You were never allowed to know about your own baby?'

And finally, finally, Grace permitted herself a sad laugh that, even to her own ears, she could hear was tinged with bitterness.

'I once told you that my parents were academics. They weren't unkind, or harsh, but they believed in rules, in studies, in application to my schoolwork. They didn't believe in frivolous toys, or days out that weren't also educational, or parties.'

She gripped the bar tighter, but Rik didn't speak. As though he was giving her time. And space.

'When I was sixteen, I went to a party. My first ever one. Two of the kids in my school threw it when their parents had gone out of town for a weekend, and their older brother was supposed to have been babysitting them.'

'You parents couldn't have agreed to that,' Rik prompted carefully, when she hesitated again. 'You didn't do parties, and that stuff. You told me you were a boring kid.'

'They didn't,' she confirmed, and even now she could almost feel the emotion of that time washing through her, all over again. 'They forbade it, of course. But I was desperate to go so I slipped out of the house. I didn't want to be the geek. The nerd. Just for one night, I wanted to be like every other normal kid. But...'

'But you met a boy, had sex, and fell pregnant,' Rik said for her, when she couldn't find the words herself.

'I was foolish, and over-excited, and I'm not really sure I knew what I was really doing. I think I even believed I couldn't possibly get pregnant the first time.'

'That was your first time?'

Her cheeks grew hot with shame.

'That was my only time,' she bit out. 'Until you.'

And she had no idea what that low, guttural sound that Rik made was, but even to Grace's untrained ear it sounded deliciously like possessiveness.

'It took me seven months to admit it even to myself,' she made herself continue. 'Hiding my growing figure with baggier and baggier clothes. But, in the end, I couldn't hide it from my parents any longer. They were horrified, of course.'

'What happened?' Rik growled, and somehow Grace felt as if it was a protective sound.

For her, rather than against her.

'My parents told me that I would have the baby adopted, they would move universities, and we would start again. So that's what happened. I had the baby—it was a girl, I know that—but I never got to hold her,' Grace admitted, though the words seared in her chest. 'My parents had her taken away and I never saw her. We never spoke of it again. We moved house. That was that.'

Rik didn't answer immediately. She got the feeling he was taking it all in. Absorbing it.

'So, why come back here if you don't even know this is where she is?' he asked eventually.

Wordlessly, Grace stared out over the blanket of lights that was Thorncroft.

'I don't know,' she admitted, after what felt like an eternity. 'Probably because this was where she was born. Being here is the closest I can ever feel to her. It's the only comfort I have.'

'What about tracking her down?' he asked. 'Putting your name on one of those databases?'

Grace gripped the railing tighter than ever.

'I've wanted to,' she confessed. 'A thousand times. But...'

She tailed off. How could she explain that terror that lodged so intently in her chest every time she came close to contacting the Adoption Contact Register. Her daughter might not be able to register herself until she was eighteen, so right now Grace could tell herself that age was the reason they had no contact.

But what if her daughter turned eighteen and still never registered? What if she never wanted to know her. It was her greatest fear- that her daughter would reject her.

'That isn't my point,' Grace bit out, abruptly changing the subject. 'My point is that I wanted you to know the truth. I wish other people knew. I've hated her being kept like some dirty secret. I just didn't know how to tell anyone...until now.'

He didn't ask why, and for that Grace was grateful. She didn't think she had an answer for that.

'I'm honoured that you did,' he said quietly.

Then, at long last, she allowed him to peel her hands from the balcony and turn her around, that dark look of his snagging hers instantly, as though there were no one else in the place. Hot, and intent, sending liquid heat pouring through her, the way that it always did when Rik was around.

And Grace had no idea how long they stood there, with his arms around her, but it was long enough to finally gather herself again.

'You know, just a few months ago—before I'd even met you—I'd decided it was time for me to stop living in the past. Time for me to let go, and finally move away from Thorncroft on my own.'

She wasn't sure he'd heard her—her voice muffled as it was against his chest—until he moved her back, his eyes searching her face.

'You want to leave Thorncroft.'

'I do.' She nodded. 'I just don't know if I was fooling myself that I could have done it. Not when it really came down to it. But, now that you're here, I don't think I need to. Maybe it could just be…a fresh start.'

His gaze changed in an instant. Almost imperceptibly, but Grace knew this man too well already not to notice it. It was a look that she didn't recognise. A look that sent a trickle of premonition down her very spine. She faltered, sure that whatever was going on in his head, she didn't want to know.

'A fresh start?'

His sympathetic tone was humiliating, and still, Grace forced herself to continue. To hear the words she didn't want him to say.

'I thought you and I…here in Thorncroft…'

'Grace.' He spared her from finishing, and though his eyes locked with hers, steely and unyielding, she thought it was the unguarded softness in his tone that wounded the deepest. 'Once my stint here with the exchange programme is done, I return to Sweden. Staying here, with you, has never been an option for me. I didn't think it was for you, either.'

Rik hated himself.

He could see the pain, and misery etched into every line on her face, and he knew that he had caused it.

What kind of a man was he to do that? Especially after she'd just shared what had to be her most private secret with him.

But what else was he to have done? He couldn't have lied to her and pretended that staying in Thorncroft was an option for him—especially not with his relationship with his brother so fractured and irreparable.

'I'm sorry,' he apologised, and he felt the weight of every syllable. 'Our time together has been good, *älskling*. And we have both shared things that we've never shared with anyone else, have we not?'

She eyed him warily, suspecting she was stepping into some kind of trap but couldn't quite see where it was.

'We have,' she muttered huskily.

'But I do not belong in Thorncroft. It isn't the place for me. It wouldn't be, even if not for the fact that my brother does not want me here.'

'And what if I want you here?' She lifted her chin defiantly. 'Does that count for nothing? Because there is something between us, Rik, you can't deny it.'

'I'm not trying to,' he heard himself agree. 'But we both know that whatever either of us might think we feel, this...*thing* between us is based on a lie.

'What are you talking about?' she whispered, as if he was punishing her for something she didn't even deserve.

As if there were a noose around her neck exactly like the one that he felt encircled his own.

'I asked you once before if you were spending time with me because you wanted to, or because my brother had asked you to keep a watch on me. I told you that it didn't matter to me either way, but that I wanted to know. I asked you to do me the decency of telling me the truth or, if you couldn't do that, at least not lying to me.'

And she wanted to deny it, he could see it in Grace's elegant face. She wanted to explain, but even though she worked her jaw, no sound actually came out.

'You told me that it had nothing to do with my brother. But that wasn't true, was it? You were running down a clock, playing me and keeping me away from him until my time at Thorncroft ran out.'

'You're wrong.' She gasped, but Rik shook his head.

'I'm not wrong. But I didn't think it mattered because I told myself that you were just a distraction. I convinced myself that it didn't matter if you were manipulating me, because I was using you, too. In the absence of my brother talking to me, you were my way towards understanding him a little better.'

She blanched, and Rik hated himself a little more.

'So…you used me,' she rasped out. Painfully.

'I told myself that I was, just as I think you told yourself that you were only with me to help my brother.'

'The difference is—' she jerked her back straighter, as if that might lend her more strength '—that the person I was fooling most of all was myself. I pretended getting close to you was a plan because it was the excuse I think I needed.'

'Maybe so, but—'

'Because, deep down, I knew I was attracted to you. I had been since that first night at the ball, before I even knew who you were. What's more…' She leaned forward and, inconceivably, poked him in the chest. Hard. 'I know you felt that same attraction.'

'Whether I did or not, it makes little difference,' he told her bleakly.

'It makes every difference,' Grace cried.

He shook his head.

'No,' he told her firmly. 'It doesn't. It doesn't matter whether this thing between us is real now, because it was all based on a lie. And my entire life has been based on lies, Grace. Lies, and deceit, and betrayal. I can't have another thing like that.'

'But this isn't. Not any more.'

'Not any more,' he echoed sadly. 'And that's exactly the point. *Any more.* Which means you know it once was, just as I do. Whatever we think we have, or could have, it's too late. It has already been tainted by the lies from the start.'

'It doesn't have to be,' Grace breathed. 'For my part in it all, I'm sorry.'

Her gaze was holding his so sincerely that he almost believed her.

Almost.

Something shifted and fractured inside him. Something he wasn't yet prepared to acknowledge.

'You have nothing to apologise for,' he bit out. 'Your loyalty to my brother is admirable. There's no need to qualify it.'

'My loyalty to your brother isn't why I slept with you.'

He opened his mouth to answer, but then Grace

edged closer to him and the familiar red-berry scent of her hair conditioner conjured up a dozen memories that stopped him in his tracks.

Desperately he tried to mentally scramble backwards, searching for some kind of purchase for his thoughts. Because as much as he hated to admit it, Grace deserved better than a man like him.

'I told you, aside from the one single time I slept with a man—boy, really—and fell pregnant, every other time was with you.' Her voice cracked. 'And do I need to remind you how many times that has been? I wouldn't have done that for anyone, not even someone I called my closest friend.'

Without warning, the truth of that statement hit Rik. And it felt like some precious, fragile gift that she'd given him. Her trust after what had to be years of feeling betrayed.

And suddenly, he felt unworthy.

Whether they'd started out using each other, or not, when it really came down to it, Grace had had a lot more to lose from it than him. Being intimate with him, when the last time she'd been intimate with anyone had been when she'd been sixteen, meant more than just words.

More than he had to offer.

He'd caused her enough harm. If he was the kind of decent man that he'd always believed himself to be, then he had to let her go.

'You were right when you once accused me of being selfish,' he ground out. 'I didn't care about your friendship with my brother, as much as I may have told myself that I did. You told me time and again that he was your friend and that you didn't want to hurt him, but I still pursued you. Because I wanted you.'

Rik had thought it would be hard to admit those truths. The fact was, once he'd started speaking they'd come out naturally.

'Is that so?'

He inhaled deeply.

'It is. I think perhaps a part of me wanted to get back at him, after all. It seems I'm not the man I wanted you to think I was.'

Without warning, Grace closed the gap between them and the heat that emanated off her body seemed to bounce straight to his. And straight to that frozen block that he thought had once been his heart.

'So you've just contradicted your own argument, Rik,' she observed. 'You were with me because you wanted to be. Anything to do with your brother was just an excuse. A sideshow.'

'No.' Had he contradicted himself?

He thought he might have.

'Yes,' Grace confirmed. 'And it's precisely that acknowledgement which makes you exactly the man you wanted me to think you are,' she murmured. 'You weren't selfish, Rik. You never were.

I was wrong to say it. What your mother did left you as damaged and closed-off as it left Bas. And why wouldn't it?'

'I stood by and let her send Bas away. My own brother.'

'Neither of you could have predicted what happened that night.'

'Perhaps not, but I should have done more.' Rik heard the self-loathing in his voice. But there was nothing he could do to stop it. 'He was my *brother.*'

'You were seven,' countered Grace, lifting her hands to his cheeks and cupping his face as though *she* wanted to provide *him* solace.

When they both knew it should have been the other way round.

'I was supposed to be the calm one. The measured brother. I should have waited for her to calm down, and then found a way to talk her around. I should never have let it happen.'

'You're asking a lot of a child,' Grace pointed out. 'Even when that child was yourself.'

'Maybe, but it informs the man I am today. And it seems I'm not as without fault as I had thought I was.'

'None of us are, Rik. But you should stay and give your brother a little longer to come to terms with it. More importantly, you should give yourself a break. How long have you been squashing this down inside? Punishing yourself to the point where you can't even give us a chance?'

'That isn't what's happening here,' Rik denied.

Only he felt twisted up in knots suddenly, unsure of exactly how he felt. The only thing he knew was that, if it hadn't been for Grace, then he would never have opened up this pit of emotions.

He just couldn't tell if that was a good or a bad thing. Either way, it didn't change one thing. The issue that had started the conversation in the first place.

'The point is that I can't stay here in Thorncroft, Grace. I have to leave. My life is in Sweden.'

'It doesn't have to be,' she countered.

'But I want it to be,' he assured her quietly. Then, before he realised what he was saying, he added, 'Come with me.'

He wasn't sure which of them was more shocked.

'To Sweden?'

'Why not?' He hunched his shoulder suddenly. It didn't sound like such a bad idea. 'You said it yourself, you were looking to leave anyway. To travel.'

'I was,' she agreed slowly. Uncertainly. 'But I can't. I can't quite let go.'

'Of the daughter who might not even be in this city? Even in this country.'

Grace hesitated before dropping her head.

'Yet she might be.'

Rik breathed slowly.

'So we're at an impasse.'

'It seems so.' She cast him a look of misery.

And even though something in his brain was telling him to fight for her—to say something— he found that he couldn't.

He'd been fighting for his brother for so long that he had nothing left. Which meant that there was nothing else for him to do but to make the right decision for both of them.

Wordlessly, Rik slipped on the rest of his clothes, gathering his wallet before heading to his suite door. The fact that she didn't say a word told him all he needed to know.

'You can leave in your own time. I'll stay at the hospital tonight.'

And before either of them could say anything more, he pulled open the door, and left.

CHAPTER THIRTEEN

'HI, KATE. I'M GRACE.' Smiling encouragement, Grace crossed the private room to where her patient was lying on the bed in labour. 'I'm here to have a look at your baby.'

She smiled again, but the truth was that it was hard to smile these days. She wasn't sure she had that first week after her break-up—for want of a better term—from Rik. The second week, she'd had to find a way to smile for her patients. And this week, it was easier to pretend.

But she certainly didn't feel it on the inside.

Who knew that having this kind of feelings for a person could leave you feeling so bare, so hollowed-out inside, once they were gone?

The only other time she'd felt like this, she'd been a young girl in a bed like this one, screaming as some nameless doctor walked out with the baby daughter she hadn't even had chance to see, let alone hold.

'The midwife said the umbilical cord is around the baby's neck,' Kate said shakily, reaching for her husband's hand for support.

'That's right,' Grace confirmed, making sure she included both worried parents. 'It's what we call a nuchal cord but, although it might sound terrifying, it's actually a very common occurrence, happening in around one in three births.'

'Won't it… I don't know…' Darren dropped his voice as he feared the word itself might harm their baby '…strangle the baby?'

Grace shook her head.

'Your baby is still getting all the oxygen and nutrients he needs through the cord, and he won't need to take a real breath until he's actually out in the world.'

'What if it gets a kink in it, like a hose?' Darren asked, as though he were speaking a foreign language, and he were having difficulty remembering how to speak it. 'How will the oxygen get through then?'

She watched as he and Kate gripped each other's hands even tighter, her heart going out to both of them.

'The umbilical cord has its own little set of tricks and skills,' she assured them. 'It's filled with a soft, gelatinous fluid—like a jelly—which protects all the vessels inside, and helps to protect against being compressed, or *kinked*.'

'Oh. So, we just…leave it?'

'Often intervention can cause more problems than if we just give the delivery chance to progress on its own. But to make sure the baby stays okay, I have this machine called a pulse oximeter device, and I'm going to insert the sensor into you, Kate, to your baby. That way I can monitor his oxygen saturation levels and ensure that he isn't in any undue distress.'

'Okay.' They both nodded quickly, exchanging a sweet, private look with each other.

For some inexplicable reason, it made Grace think of Rik. She shoved the errant thought from her head.

But their relationship hadn't been real, had it? Not like the couple in front of her.

She and Rik had only been together in the first place because they had a mutual connection in Bas. Rik wouldn't have bothered with her if not for his brother, and she would never have asked him to help at the charity fete if Bas hadn't demanded it.

Except that the attraction between her and Rik had been there from that first night at the gala— before they'd known they had Bas in common.

She concentrated on the task in hand.

'These are good oxygen saturation levels, Kate,' Grace encouraged her patient as she checked the results. 'Your baby is doing well.'

Still, the worry niggled at her. The baby had its umbilical cord wrapped around its neck and its position made it impossible to reach in and free it. On the positive side, it wasn't so tight that it was causing the baby's heart rate to plummet with each contraction, but that could change at any time. Not that there was any point scaring the understandably anxious parents with that detail.

The door opened just as she was checking the clock. It was the midwife she'd assigned to Naomi Fox, beckoning her. Grace dipped her head in acknowledgement and returned her focus back to her current patient. Half an hour longer for the delivery to progress, all the while monitoring the baby, and if Kate hadn't delivered by then, they might have to consider other intervention methods.

Quietly, she relayed the information to the midwives assigned to the couple, and told them to find her if anything changed, then she slipped out of the door into the pristine hallway of the Jansen wing, where her other colleague was waiting for her.

'Where are we with Naomi?' Grace asked quietly. 'Is the OR free yet?'

'Yes, they're prepping it now and we're ready to start taking her through.'

A combination of relief and unease washed over Grace.

'Is anyone on the way?'

Naomi and Bas had been utterly discreet through the pregnancy so far—with Bas following Naomi's request for him to keep away whilst she went for her weekly foetal non-stress test, even though Grace knew it had near killed him.

But given the shock results of today's test, surely Naomi had called him to alert him to what was going on.

So much for hoping for a baseline foetal heart rate of around one hundred and twenty, to one hundred and sixty—when the results had started to emerge, it had been clear that Naomi was having contractions and that the baby was beginning to look as though it might be struggling.

If the baby went into foetal distress, she would have no choice but to deliver via caesarean section. Yet if she delivered the baby without Bas being present, he would never forgive her.

But what was she to do? Ultimately, Naomi was her patient. Not her friend.

'Her sister should be here any minute,' the midwife told her, oblivious to the turmoil in Grace's head.

Clearly the two of them must have had some kind of falling out, if Naomi was contacting her sister instead of Bas, and the knowledge affected Grace far more than it had any right to.

She'd really begun to believe in them as a couple. The idea that Bas might have been able to overcome his demons and be with the mother of his soon-to-be-born baby had been somehow buoying.

As though, if he could achieve that much, then perhaps there was hope for her, too.

And perhaps even for her and Rik.

She'd picked up the phone half a dozen times, but never placed the call.

She'd even sat in her car in the road outside his hotel. But then she'd driven away again.

There wasn't a single part of her that didn't ache to tell him how badly she yearned for him.

With a deep breath, Grace nodded briefly to her colleague, headed into the next corridor to Naomi's room, and opened the door.

'I'm in labour, Bas.' She heard Naomi's agonised voice. 'And I couldn't even feel it.'

But it was the fact that Bas was standing there, one hand enveloping Naomi's, the other stroking the hair off her forehead, that filled Grace with relief.

Whatever Naomi had done, it seemed that her sister had at least had the presence of mind to call Bas, after all. Still, he didn't even notice Grace as she made her way to the cardiotocograph to check the recent results.

'That's not uncommon,' Grace said quietly, not wanting to intrude on her friend's moment, but needing to do her job. 'With all the fluid, and the discomfort you've been feeling up to this point.'

'So, bed rest?' Bas cut in, his voice sounding so different from his usual, unflappable self. 'You can give her something to stop the contractions, Grace. Betamimetics? Try to keep the baby in just a little longer. Preferably to at least thirty-seven weeks.'

'Her cervix is already beginning to change and your little one isn't tolerating the contractions too well.' Grace shook her head as she glanced at Bas, then looked back at Naomi. 'We'll prep you for a C-section now, Naomi.'

'I'm coming in.' Bas lifted the side of the bed, clearly readying himself to move it.

As if he were the surgeon, rather than her patient's partner.

'You'll wait here,' Grace told him firmly. 'I'll take good care of her, Bas. But you're the father right now, not the surgeon. I'll make sure we call you as soon as she's prepped.'

He glowered at her, but she stood firm. This was her area of expertise, and he needed to trust. They both knew it—however much Bas might have desperately needed to feel in control at that moment.

'Go,' he grunted at last, dipping his head to kiss Naomi's forehead.

Solicitous. Loving. It was so unlike the Bas that she'd known all these years—and yet not.

Just as Rik had said.

But there was no time to dwell. With a gentle word to Bas as she ushered him into the chair—not that she thought he heard her—she instructed her team to get Naomi up and on her feet. It was better for her and the baby if she kept moving, and it was only a brief walk to the delivery OR, just down the corridor.

And then she began prepping Naomi for the

C-section, all the while talking to her, and reassuring her as much as possible.

By the time one of her team had gone to get Bas gowned up and brought in, she had Naomi in the OR and in place. And before Naomi was wheeled out—cradling her magnificently strong newborn, who they'd just named Aneka, before she would be taken to NICU—Bas stepped towards Grace.

'Thank you.'

'Any time,' she told him, half choked up despite her wide smile.

Because this was the moment she'd never had the chance to experience with her own daughter. It was the reason why she'd never been able to move on.

Which meant that Rik was right about tracking her down—she needed that connection.

Or that closure.

'I was surprised to receive your call,' Rik told his brother as they stood, finally facing one another without being over a patient.

Though *surprised* didn't quite cover the shock he'd felt when—right in the middle of packing his bags for his last day in the UK—his phone had rung with an unknown number.

He'd taken the call straight away. In hindsight he'd been hoping it had been Grace. He could never have predicted it would have been his brother, ringing to ask him to meet before he left for the airport.

So now, he was here in the hospital coffee shop. Presumably, Bas didn't want to leave the grounds whilst the mother of his baby was still recovering. He'd heard the rumours, of course. How the playboy surgeon Bas Jansen had become a father a few days earlier.

It was all a far cry from the reunion he'd spent decades envisaging. But then, he'd long since given up on that. That dream had paled into significance when he'd lost Grace—the woman he'd never expected to crash his life.

He eyed his brother. A few weeks ago, the animosity had been clear in every line of his Bas's body. Every black look shot from his ice-cold eyes. Now, Rik couldn't help but notice, his brother seemed different.

Changed.

No doubt due to the baby that the entire hospital was talking about—as well as the woman who had allegedly finally tamed him.

'Let's get on with this, shall we?' Bas suggested.

But that, too, lacked the bitter heat from weeks before.

'How is fatherhood?' Rik asked, surprising even himself.

He didn't know if he'd thought his brother would answer, but then Bas's chest actually began to swell with pride before Rik's eyes and, abruptly, Rik realised that it was Naomi, and his new baby, who had somehow effected this reunion. Not Grace, as he'd initially thought.

He wasn't sure what that meant.

'Fine,' Bas began in a clipped voice, but then he clearly couldn't help himself. 'I never thought I would ever be a parent, yet I've learned how to be a father. A proper father. I've begun to understand what it is to love, and to accept love.'

'And you didn't know that before?' Rik demanded before he could swallow the words down.

His brother's face darkened.

'How could I know?' he demanded. 'I had no idea what love felt like. It's taken me until now to understand it.'

'Then I envy you,' was all Rik could manage.

'You envy me? Are you completely deluded?'

And there it was. The truth that had been hanging over Rik for so long.

'I always envied you. You got away.'

'I got away?' his brother echoed angrily. 'I was the one who envied you.'

Rik frowned. It made no sense.

'I can't imagine why,' he bit out.

And his brother erupted.

'You had it all. You were the one she wanted— the one she heaped love onto—whilst I was the one she cast aside.'

'Say that again,' Rik demanded slowly, his tone

unexpectedly dangerous, but his brother didn't seem to heed it.

In the back of his mind, Rik heard Grace's voice, telling him just how wounded Bas had been by the events of that night.

He hadn't really listened to her, though, he'd been too caught up in everything he himself had lost that night.

'You were the one she wanted to keep, whilst I was the one she couldn't wait to get rid of.'

This was insane, Rik reflected darkly. His brother had completely twisted up events to suit his agenda. He couldn't possibly remember it that way.

'Have you seriously forgotten what it was like in that house when things didn't go our stepfather's way?' Rik demanded, his voice suddenly hoarse. 'Did you consider that, with you gone, I was the only punchbag left? Did you think she'd suddenly stop turning a blind eye to his tempers?'

'That was your decision. You're the one who told authorities I was lying when I'd had enough. At least she wanted to keep you. I got sent to be with a father who never wanted me around.'

'You can't really mean that?'

Things churned inside him. Dark and forbidding. He could hardly take in what he was hearing, but his brother gritted his teeth at him as though he truly believed it.

'How do you think it feels to be the son so

awful that even his mother couldn't love him?' Bas rasped. 'I spent years wondering what was so wrong…so flawed about me, that wasn't you. You were always the perfect son.'

'That's…preposterous.' Rik suddenly found himself trying to control his temper from the sheer absurdity of it.

How could his brother possibly believe that, after all that had happened in the lead up to that night?

After everything he himself had done, stepping in to take the next beating because, after the night before, he'd been afraid their stepfather might actually kill Bas this time.

But his brother leaned back, folding his arms over his chest defensively.

'That's the truth. The last words she told me were that you and I might be twins, but that I lacked your compassionate side. That I was a horrid little bastard who no one could ever love.'

'Is that what you truly think?' Rik laughed, but even to his own ears it was a hollow, cold sound.

'Is that the way you remember things in your head, Basilius? That she somehow favoured me?'

'Didn't she?' his brother demanded.

'No,' Rik snapped. 'Our mother was a master of manipulation. She used to tell me that I lacked the kind of personality that you had. She told me that I was a pathetic excuse for a boy, and that no one could ever love me.'

Neither of them spoke for a moment. Hadn't he accused Grace of that—of having manipulated him—the last time they'd spoken? How could he have equated the two? He felt sick just thinking about it.

Had he really failed to appreciate just how much she'd come to mean to him, even in the short time they'd had?

But now wasn't the time for analysing his relationship with Grace.

Rik pressed on.

'Have you really forgotten what our mother was truly like? Have you forgotten how she used to play one of us against the other? Always trying to drive that wedge between us? All for attention?'

'I haven't forgotten anything,' Bas ground out. 'I remember how she more than loved attention, she *craved* it. She couldn't live without it. Attention to her was like air is to every other normal human being. Without it, she might as well be suffocating, dying. And you gave it to her.'

'I was trying to keep her sweet.' Rik shook his head. 'In a good mood. Especially when *he* came along, and it went from her manipulation to his fists.'

'You never really bore the brunt of that, did you?' Bas said, and Rik thought it might have been intended as a dig, but in reality it came out with such anguish that it might as well have reached into his chest and squeezed.

'Not as much as you did. I know that,' Rik murmured. 'You made sure of it.'

He paused, waiting for his brother to reply, but Bas didn't. His expression was strange, as though he barely even recalled that.

'Don't you remember how you would take the blame for me?' Rik demanded, confused. 'Taking responsibility for things I was supposed to have done wrong, even though you'd had nothing to do with it? If we were out of milk. If a light had been left on. Even simply if we walked down the stairs the wrong way.'

'I remember all that,' Bas began, 'but I don't remember taking the blame for you.'

And then it struck Rik—the reason that Bas didn't remember things the way that he did. How ironic that he himself had forgotten.

'Well, you did.' Rik dipped his head in a curt nod. 'Almost all the time. You were always a protector, Basilius. Even for me. The only reason you didn't try to protect me that day was because you were concussed. Not that either of us understood that at the time.'

'Say that again?'

'You got walloped the day before. Only, it was so rough that you'd actually been sick. You told me that everything had gone black. If it hadn't been for that, you would have leaped in for me again. The way you always did.'

Bas glowered at him. But there was a flickering in his eyes, as though he was desperately trying to remember. Rik wished Grace were here, though whether for himself or for his brother, he couldn't be certain.

'So why did you betray me?' Bas demanded abruptly. 'Why did you back her up, that final time, instead of me?'

Rik eyed him incredulously. Had the concussion been so bad that he'd forgotten everything?

No wonder Grace had believed he had wronged his brother. No wonder Bas hadn't wanted to make contact with him all these years, if that was what he honestly thought. But now it was finally chance to set things right.

'Because we agreed that was what I was going to do,' Rik bit out simply.

He might have known his brother wouldn't believe him.

'What are you talking about?' Bas ground out. 'Why would we ever, *ever* agree that?'

Inside, Rik felt raw. Scraped hollow. And the things that moved within him were too dark, and angry, and frustrated.

'You really don't remember?'

'Remember what?'

Rik eyed him grimly. No wonder people never

wanted to rehash a bad past. It stirred up too many unwanted ghosts. And too many *what ifs*.

'We agreed that if Child Welfare took us, then they'd probably end up splitting us up. We didn't want that.'

'That conversation never happened,' Bas scorned. 'Besides, we got split up anyway.'

'How could we have foreseen that?' demanded Rik. 'We didn't know Magnus existed. We didn't even know that deadbeat wasn't our father.'

Bas shook his head, his expression thunderous.

'So that's what you're claiming? That was our plan? That we agreed I would tell the truth, only for you to back up our mother's lie? I don't think much of that so-called plan.'

'Our plan was that we would get rid of Child Welfare, and then we were going to run away and find Mrs P. And Bertie,' Rik fired back, just about controlling his temper. 'You really don't remember?'

'I don't remember because it didn't happen.'

'It must have been the concussion,' Rik pointed out.

And he could see that his brother hated that it made sense.

Hated it, and something else. Something that Rik could only hope was *welcoming it*.

'You're saying you told them that I was lying so that they would go away?'

Rik couldn't tell whether his brother was finally beginning to see it, or not. Still, he kept trying.

He had to. He hadn't been searching for decades to simply give up because his brother didn't take his word for it.

The way he shouldn't have given up on Grace.

'And we wouldn't be torn apart before we'd had chance to escape and find Mrs P.'

The two men stood in contemplative silence. And finally, *finally* it seemed that his brother was listening to him.

'I tried to find you,' Rik offered, after one silence bled into another. 'But I had no idea where to start looking or how. I asked, but she never told me anything, of course.'

'I find that harder to believe. Even back then, Magnus Jansen had made a name for himself as a surgeon.'

Rik cast him a long look, but he knew he had to be open with his brother.

Grace had shown him that much.

'Up until our mother's death, before Christmas last year, I thought my name was Henrik Magnusson. I've spent a decade looking up every Magnusson in Sweden. I had no idea you were even in the UK, let alone that I should really be looking for the name Jansen. The only thing I ever gleaned from her, growing up, was that he was a surgeon. It was the one nugget I held onto. So damned tightly. My one connection to you.'

'So much so that you became a surgeon?' Bas rasped.

'Yes.'

So simple. So frank. It clearly rattled Bas—the idea that he might have got it all wrong, all these years.

'You expect me to believe that you only found out the truth when our mother told you...what, on her deathbed?'

'I can't tell you what to believe, Basilius. I can only tell you the facts as I know them to be. And she didn't tell me anything, whether on her deathbed or otherwise. Finally telling the truth would have been too kind an ending for her, Basilius. She was bitter and vengeful until the end.'

'Then how?' Bas bit out.

'When she died, Mrs P saw the obituary in the paper and made contact. When I told her what had happened all those years ago, she was able to fill in some of the gaps. Once I pieced it together with what I knew, I was able to find you.'

Bas looked as if he'd just taken a body blow. And Rik felt as if he'd just landed one.

'Mrs P is still out there?' he whispered.

'She is.'

'And Bertie?'

A sadness shot through Rik.

'He died. About a decade ago. Apparently, they'd both been waiting. Hoping we would one day seek them out.'

'They didn't seek us out,' Bas gritted out, as though he didn't care.

But Rik knew better. He was beginning to recognise the brother he'd once known. The brother he'd missed, all these years.

'They didn't know where we'd gone, Basilius. And they didn't want to risk causing problems for us when we were younger. They'd hoped that with them out of the picture, our mother's jealousy would have dissipated. And when we never got in touch, they let themselves believe it.'

Bas grunted but didn't speak.

'She would love to know about you and Naomi. I can only imagine how much joy it would bring her to hear about your new baby girl.'

With a start, his brother jerked his hand up for Rik to stop, clearly needing a moment to try to make sense of it all.

But Rik couldn't afford to let him. He still had to leave for his flight, and he couldn't risk his brother shutting down again. This was his one chance.

'You seem to think you have the monopoly on being rejected, *bror*. On being mistreated, and wronged. But, from my perspective, you got the better deal. You got away from her. And maybe Magnus wasn't any more welcoming, or loving, I can't speak to that,' Henrik rasped, 'but at least his fists were never the answer.'

Bas glowered at him as though he thought it was his own fault.

'How long did you stay?'

'I got away when I was fifteen,' Rik told him bleakly. 'Then, as soon as I could, I joined the army and I got my education that way.'

He couldn't bring himself to say any more. Not yet. Not when he hadn't even told Grace any of it.

And he'd had the gall to accuse her of not being open and honest with him.

'What about him?' Bas asked abruptly. 'Where is he now?'

Rik scoffed.

He shrugged. 'Who knows? Without you or me there as a punchbag, he turned his attention onto her. She saw her chance to take him to court for compensation and she divorced him.'

His brother's face said it all.

Erin Sundberg had been prepared to stay with the man even when he'd hurt her kids, but it had been different when she herself had become the target. He couldn't imagine caring that little for his kids—it was why he'd never planned on having any. But now, looking at his brother—a new father himself—he couldn't imagine Bas ever letting anyone lay a finger on his child.

Did that mean there was hope, after all? For him and for Grace? He'd let her go because he'd thought he couldn't love anyone. He'd thought he wasn't capable.

Now he knew that he was.

Perhaps he ought to fight for Grace with half the drive that he'd fought for his brother all these years.

'*Bror*, I need your help with something.'

CHAPTER FOURTEEN

'WHERE ARE WE GOING?' Grace asked Rik, as they strode along the busy pavement in the tourist-popular side of town.

'Think of it as my last gift to you, before I leave for Sweden,' Rik answered, which she couldn't help thinking was no answer at all. 'My apology, and my goodbye, all wrapped into one. You look perfect by the way. Beautiful.'

Self-consciously, she smoothed her hands over her caramel fitted trousers, and cream fine-knit jumper. He hadn't said where their date—not that this was a date—was going to be, so she'd thought it the safest option. Smart but casual.

As if what she wore could change the fact that he was leaving. That he'd invited her to join him. Or that, despite every fibre in her body wanting to, Grace couldn't quite break that one final, probably imagined tie to Thorncroft.

Lost in her own head, Grace almost stumbled when Rik stopped abruptly outside a little café and ushered her inside. Then, after a brief glance around, he led them both to a table.

And Grace couldn't have said why her heart kicked up a beat as she sat down, her eyes darting everywhere whilst she waited for him to speak—

which he clearly didn't intend to do until after they'd ordered their drinks.

The wait seemed interminably long. And then, at last, Rik began.

'I spoke with my brother the other day.'

'I heard.' Grace nodded, taking a careful sip of her hot drink. 'Though that's all I know. He and Naomi, and their baby, have been in their own private bubble ever since the birth. It's lovely to see.'

'I think they'll be fine. I saw more of the brother I used to know.'

'So you reconciled?' A kind of happiness swelled in her chest, though she couldn't have said if it was for Rik, or for her friend. Or both.

'I think it's safe to say that we've started to. It will take time, but I believe we're on our way.'

'I'm happy for you.'

'I know that you are,' Rik agreed, without hesitation.

'So, does that mean you'll be staying after all?'

And what did it say that her chest tightened at the idea, almost willing him to say *yes*? Where did she think anything could possibly lead, whilst she was so paralysed in Thorncroft?

'The invitation to join me is still there.'

'Thank you,' she whispered, wishing more than anything that she had the courage to do just that. 'I wish I could.'

Unexpectedly, Rik laid his hand over hers.

'It's down to you,' he told her softly.

And Grace wished it were that easy.

'Rik…' she began, then faltered.

But he made her feel stronger when he reached out and lifted her chin with his finger. Making her look at him. Holding her gaze with his own.

'At some point in the next ten minutes, your daughter will walk through that door.'

Something walloped into Grace's body—so hard that it stole the breath from her very lungs.

'Don't panic.' He squeezed her hand tightly. 'This isn't an engineered meeting. You aren't here to meet her. I'm giving you the chance to leave now, if that's what you want.'

'Why would you…?'

'I'm just showing you that you were right coming back to Thorncroft—she has been here all along.'

And everything was too tight in Grace's body, in her head, to speak. But it didn't matter, because Rik was answering all those clamouring, unspoken questions.

'She reached out to the adoption agency a few years ago, along with her adopted mother's approval. So she wants to know who you are. This is their family café. It's amazing what my wealth, and my brother's contacts in this city, can unearth.'

'You told your brother?'

It was probably the least important question right now, but it was all she could voice. Emotions were bombarding her. Too many of them, and too heavy-hitting for her to identify.

'You once told me that you wished other people knew about your daughter. That you hated her being kept like some dirty secret, but that you just didn't know how to tell anyone.'

Grace nodded, not trusting herself to speak.

'Do you want us to go?' he checked, after a while.

Her head swam. She wasn't ready to meet her daughter, but she didn't want to leave, either.

'She doesn't know I'm here?'

'She doesn't have the slightest clue about you. I brought you here to try to help you the way that you helped me with my own brother. To give you the nudge you need to either go home and sign that register, or to walk away for good. Because you can't go on as you are now, with your life in limbo. Believe me, I know how it feels.'

It was as if his every word was lodging in her head. And it was everything she'd wanted to tell herself but hadn't had the courage to do in the past. Not alone.

But this time, she wasn't alone. Rik was right here with her. So Grace waited, not even sure if she kept remembering to breathe. Every second ticking loudly in her head, echoing its countdown.

And then, suddenly, the door opened and there was no doubting that the young girl who walked through that door was the daughter she'd given birth to. It was like looking into a mirror straight back to her past.

The girl was a carbon copy of the fourteen-year-old Grace herself had been.

'That's…her…?' she managed to whisper, to no one in particular, though she gripped Rik's hand tighter.

'That's her,' he confirmed quietly.

Tears burned her eyes, her throat constricting, and Grace watched, transfixed, as the girl bounced across the room, dropped a kiss on the cheek of the woman who had served them, and then slid behind the counter to make herself a drink. A thick, frothy, strawberry milkshake by the look of it. And all the while, the girl chatted non-stop to the woman who was obviously her adopted mother.

Her real mum, Grace reminded herself.

Because that woman was the one who had raised her to be such a joyous, fun, secure young person.

'She looks…happy,' Grace managed to choke out, as something lifted off her chest.

It felt suspiciously like relief, though she'd never realised it had been squatting there all these years. Heavy and suffocating.

And it was impossible to stop the hot tears from breaking free and tracking down her face. She dashed at them impatiently.

'She's beautiful.'

'Do you want to know her name?'

'Her name?'

Grace flickered her eyes to Rik for a scant second, then back at the girl.

'They called her Amelia. Mellie for short.'

'Mellie.' Grace rolled the name around her mouth. 'It suits her.'

Everything suited her. She was the most beautiful girl Grace thought she'd ever seen in her life. And what was more, she was happy and healthy.

Surely there was nothing more perfect, more… *right* than that?

'We need to leave.' She snatched her hand out of Rik's abruptly, her heart pounding so loudly in her chest that it felt like the longest, most ominous roll of thunder. *'Now.'*

Snatching her bag up, and her coat, Grace stood as quickly as she could. She could barely keep from running as she headed for the door. But once she was outside on the pavement, amongst the bustle of the city traffic and the jostling of pedestrians, she turned and scurried, dodging people and flying across junctions.

And when Rik finally caught up with her—finally made her stop and catch a breath—she couldn't have said where she was or how far she'd gone.

Looking up into his concerned expression, Grace choked back a racking sob.

'I got it all wrong.'

'Got what wrong?' he asked gently. Steady-ingly.

Doubling over, her hands braced against her knees, she fought to steady her breathing.

'I got it wrong, and my parents got it right.' She shook her head. 'All these years, I've hated them for taking my daughter away from me. But look at her. She's happy. And loved. And perfect.'

'All the things you've always wanted for her,' Rik pointed out. 'I know you better than you think, Grace.'

Slowly, she craned her neck to look up at him.

'All the things I've wanted for her,' she agreed. 'And more. So much more.'

'Surely that's good?'

Grace sucked in a breath.

'More than I could have given her,' she man-aged. Breathing heavily into the silence for sev-eral seconds. 'That love she had with her mother, that affection. I couldn't have given her that.'

'Of course you could, though that isn't what today is meant to be about.'

'No.' She shook her head. 'I couldn't. I told you, my parents loved me in their own way, but they didn't show affection. There were no dropped kisses. No spontaneous hugs. I'd forgotten how sterile it was until I saw Mellie in there with her mother. Her *real* mother. Not me. I'm just the kid who gave birth to her.'

'Grace—'

'My childhood wasn't full of affection.' She cut him off, finally standing up and drawing in lungfuls of fresh air. 'It was a little cold, and I would have been a cold mother, too. It was really only during my career that I started to see how loving couples could be. How close families could be. Mellie is exactly where she needed to be, and my parents knew that.'

'Grace…'

'I don't know who I am any more, Rik,' she blurted out suddenly, as a huge wave of regret crashed over her. 'I don't know what I believe.'

'This was supposed to help you,' he told her, his confusion clear. 'It was about making you feel better about the choices that were made on your behalf. It wasn't supposed to make you feel worse.'

'And it does make me feel better,' she told him. 'In one way. I'm glad that she has such a loving family…'

'There's a *but*?' he demanded, as though he couldn't quite believe it.

A profound sadness opened up inside her.

'Not for her,' Grace tried to explain. 'But for me. For just how wrong I had it in my mind. For the fact that I hated my parents for taking her from me, yet that was what has given her a better life than I ever could.'

'You were sixteen,' Rik pointed out. 'And perhaps if they had handled it differently…talked to you, allowed you to talk about her…it might have been different.'

'Perhaps,' she conceded. 'But I'll never know. What I *do* know is that I'm not sure who I am any more. And maybe that sounds crazy to you—'

'It doesn't,' he cut in instantly. And she was grateful for it. 'I understand better than most how family, separations, losses, are all inextricably linked with who we are. They're some of the things that give us our sense of self.'

He was so kind and understanding. More than she thought she deserved.

'I feel like I've lost all of that,' Grace confessed. 'Like I don't know what to do next.'

'Don't rush it,' he advised. 'Take some time to think things through. I'm here with you, whenever you need me.'

Rik had intended it to give her the nudge she needed to decide one way or another but, suddenly, she felt more paralysed than ever.

'What I need…' Grace tailed off, willing the pain in her chest, and in her head, to subside. Hardly surprised when it didn't.

Every fibre of her was screaming out in protest, but she forced herself on, all the same.

'What I need,' she tried again, 'is to do this for myself. On my own.'

The look that Rik cast her was pure torture.

'You need to get some space, and clear your head,' he ground out, his arms reaching for her.

She nodded wordlessly, wishing that her body didn't melt so easily at his mere touch.

'So come with me to Sweden. You said you were ready to leave Thorncroft, and there's nothing but space and fresh air at my cabin.'

'And you,' she pointed out quietly.

'Does that matter?'

It did, because Rik was now crowding her head as much as anyone. She'd thought she'd loved him. It turned out she didn't really know how to love. Because wasn't love about doing the thing that was best for the other person? And it turned out that her cold, affectionless parents had a better idea of doing the right thing for someone else— for that little girl who had been her baby—than she herself had ever had.

It made Grace feel useless. And rejected. And then, because she felt that she ought to be happy that her daughter didn't need her, and hadn't missed her, it made her feel guilty.

'I need to work out who I am,' she managed. 'And I have to do it alone.'

For an agonisingly long moment, Rik watched her, and she lost count of the number of times words leapt into her mouth and she nearly opened her mouth and took it all back.

But she didn't. And then, with an abrupt nod, Rik conveyed his acceptance.

And Grace didn't know how she felt about the fact that he found it so easy to let her go.

* * *

Rik finally closed up on his patient after a long operation to re-excise and widen the tumour bed on a man who had previously had an unplanned excision.

The full-contrast MRI had offered him a clear image of the tumour bed and surrounding tissues, and his choice of contralateral micro-anastomosis had been the optimal decision.

But the simple truth was that these days he was grateful for every surgery that helped him to take his mind off *her*.

Grace.

It had been three months since he'd come back to Sweden, and it felt like the longest three months of his life. The need to fight for her that final day had been almost overwhelming. Rik still didn't know how he'd managed to restrain himself.

He'd only known that he'd *had* to.

He who had grown accustomed to having to fight for everything that he wanted. He was used to hunting it down with the kind of dogged determination that his years in the army had taught him. That his decades of searching for his brother had taught him.

To never give up.

So taking that step back to afford Grace the time, and space, that she'd told him she needed had probably been the hardest thing he'd ever had to do. A part of him had needed to fight, more than anything, so that the woman he'd come to realise he loved didn't have to do it alone.

But things hadn't been about what he needed. They had been about what Grace needed. And having him fight for her, or chase her down, wasn't what she'd needed at all.

So he'd sat back and waited for her—was still waiting for her—and all he could do was hope that she would, ultimately, return to him.

And though he and Bas had talked twice, over video call, their conversations had focussed mainly on his beautiful new daughter. They hadn't spoken much about Grace, but one thing his brother had said had been to remind Rik of the adage that Mrs P had once taught them—the one that said *If you love someone set them free...*

It had never been Rik's way, but somehow— even though it had damned near killed him—he'd managed to be patient. To give Grace time.

So, when he scrubbed out and headed for his consultation room, the last person he expected to see waiting inside was Grace.

For a moment, he thought perhaps he was hallucinating. And then, closing the door quietly behind him, he prowled slowly across the room, pretending to himself that he wasn't drinking her in.

She wore a pair of inky-blue jeans, which clung oh-so-lovingly to her curves, and a V-neck tee, which flattered her torso perfectly. It wasn't the usual polished version of her that he had grown accustomed to.

This Grace was somehow different. Softer. He might even have said more comfortable in her own skin.

Although one thing hadn't changed. The sight of her still made his hands itch to lift the hemline of her tee and reacquaint himself with the glorious body that lay beneath. As if he were some kind of untried kid.

He almost gave in to it. Instead, he schooled himself to hold his nerve.

'You're here,' he observed, his voice more controlled than he felt inside.

'I'm here,' she agreed, her husky voice abrading him as she edged closer.

It was like being caught in a rip tide, dragging him under no matter how hard he fought to try to reach the surface.

Although he wasn't sure he tried that hard.

He wanted her with such an intensity that he thought he might drown in that need alone. But he had to know. He had to understand exactly why she was here.

For now? Or for good?

'I finally met Amelia,' she told him, her eyes shining. So bright that he thought it might be enough to blind him. 'She's incredible.'

'She's your daughter.'

'No.' Grace shook her head, but this time there

wasn't the same sadness as back in Thorncroft. 'Not really. She is her mum and dad's daughter. They're the people who raised her. But she wanted to know me—apparently her mother was adopted as a child, too, but she found out when she was eighteen and it had been a shock to her. So she's always been up front with Mellie about being adopted, and she encouraged her daughter to reach out to her birth mother—to me.'

'So meeting her was...the right thing?' he checked.

'It was.' Grace bobbed her head. 'She has a wonderful life, and a supportive family. She doesn't need a second mum. But she does want to know me. They all do. And I want to be as much a part of her life as she will let me.'

Which meant that Grace was only here for *now*, Rik realised abruptly. And something cracked in his chest.

He smiled—and who cared if it was tight?

'You seem different,' he managed, at length.

'Do I?' She offered a light shrug. 'I've been on a bit of a round-the-world trip—someone once told me that I should take the time to discover myself more—and I've visited so many of the places I always dreamed of seeing.'

That caught him by surprise.

'You've been around the world?'

'Well, not exactly.' She gave a rueful laugh. 'My neighbour has Cooper for the moment, and

I've only been to about fifteen countries so far, in sixty days.'

'You've been travelling like you always wanted,' he realised. So was that what her neighbour had meant when she'd said Grace had gone away. One of the few things that his brother *had* told him. 'But you didn't give notice at the hospital?'

'I came to an agreement. Magnus had me work in various places he knew as part of a Jansen ambassadorial project that he's apparently been wanting to set up for a while. I've been working in a mobile hospital in India, an orphanage in Cambodia, a women's clinic on Vietnam. I have quite the résumé if you need to see it.'

She was teasing him, and he wasn't sure how he felt about that.

'So you've been travelling the world? On your own?'

'I needed to work out who I am again. Like you said…' she exhaled '… Amelia is happy, but she doesn't need me. It's time for me to finally move on and live the life I want to. And that isn't in Thorncroft. So I put together my list of places to go, and I went.'

'And now you're here,' he growled, trying to decide what to make of it.

'I am.'

'How long for?'

'I was walking over the Golden Bridge in Vietnam when I suddenly realised I had no one to share it with. And when I thought about it, I realised that the only person I wanted to share it with is you.'

'No,' he bit out, 'you don't.'

Grace simply smiled.

'I promise you, Rik, I know what I want. I've taken the time to realise who I am now—just like you said I should.'

'Grace—'

'And guess what?' She refused to let him interrupt her. 'I found the place I most wanted to see was some log cabin in the Tyresta National Park. Do you know anyone who can be my guide?'

Rik wasn't sure he was still breathing. He kept telling himself to get a grip. Because if he lost himself in those hooded eyes, and that sensuous mouth, he wasn't sure any map or compass could help him navigate his way out.

And he didn't want to deal with losing her all over again when she left.

'Why are you really here, Grace?'

'I came here for you, of course.'

So direct, and so uncomplicated. Something deep within Rik cleaved in two.

He wanted fervently to believe her but, after the childhood he'd endured, it felt almost too good to be true.

He had to be sure.

She looked up at him, and the sincerity in her expression moved right through him. Shaking him, like tectonic plates shifting. Emotions jumbled and rose within him, before dropping into a dark abyss and disappearing. And then, suddenly, something else began to rise up. Something new. *Hope.*

'I don't know if I can give you everything you deserve. I don't know if I'm capable of real love.'

'You are,' she assured him quietly. 'You had it for your brother. It's what made you sacrifice the one person you held dearest all those years ago. And it's what drove you on to find him, for all those years. You're more capable of love than you think. So, I've begun to learn, am I.'

Grace eyed him steadily. That sparkle in her eyes doing things to him and making that ache in his chest press in on him even harder.

'And since we're on the subject of love, I don't want it from anybody else. I never have done. Before you came along, I thought the only thing that really mattered was my career. You changed all that. You alone.'

Rik reached out and took her shoulders, pulling her into him. His voice so gruff that he barely recognised himself.

'I should caution you that if we start this thing, I don't know that I'll ever want to let you go.'

'I think that, by definition, is real love,' Grace returned.

So sure. So confident. And it was that light shining from her beautiful eyes, that *love*, that began to find its way to convince him.

'How long are you planning on staying?' he asked harshly.

Because he didn't know if he could bear to hear the answer. He needn't have worried.

'As long as you want me,' she told him, without a hint of uncertainty.

'What if I want you for ever?'

'Then I'd have to make sure you'd want Cooper for ever, too. I've no plans on leaving him with my neighbour for good.'

'I have a back yard perfect for twenty Coopers,' he assured her. 'Because I think, with you to guide me, *älskling*, there may be hope for me, after all.'

'There is if you want it.'

He shook his head in disbelief.

'You make it sound so easy.'

'It is so easy,' she stated with certainty. 'But also…it isn't. It's hard. Sometimes we'll disagree, maybe row. Things definitely won't always go smoothly. Sometimes things will be tough. The trick will be to hold on, and to work through it. Together. It will take a certain kind of strength, but I know you have that, because it's what brought you to this point.'

'You aren't selling this,' he teased.

But Grace continued as if she hadn't heard.

'The most important point is that it will be worth it. *We* will be worth it. And I want you to hold onto that, Rik. Because as long as you love me, it will all be worthwhile.'

'I want to be able to,' he told her sincerely. 'I want all of that.'

'Then that's all there is.'

And a thousand things moved through him at that.

'Not *all* there is,' he managed, hoarsely.

'No?'

She looked confused and he loved the idea of catching her unawares. His clever, kind, beautiful Grace.

'No,' he told her, his voice sincere. 'I think I also need to show you every day just how much I love you. How much I intend to keep loving you.'

She looked at him, her eyes raking his for meaning. He knew the precise moment she realised, and that pretty flush began to stain her smooth face.

'How much, for that matter,' he continued, 'I intend to worship you.'

'I think I would like that.' Her voice cracked, and it was like a lick of heat against his very sex. 'Very much.'

And with that, Rik cupped her face in his hands, lowered his head to claim hers—and proceeded to show her exactly how much he intended to worship her.

Every single day.

* * * * *

If you missed the previous story in the Billionaire Twin Surgeons duet, then check out

Shock Baby for the Doctor

If you enjoyed this story, check out these other great reads from Charlotte Hawkes

Tempted by Her Convenient Husband
Reunited with His Long-Lost Nurse
The Doctor's One Night to Remember

All available now!